John Dawson Ross

Bonnie Jean

A collection of Papers and Poems Relating to the Wife of Robert Burns

John Dawson Ross

Bonnie Jean
A collection of Papers and Poems Relating to the Wife of Robert Burns

ISBN/EAN: 9783744720663

Printed in Europe, USA, Canada, Australia, Japan

Cover: Foto ©Andreas Hilbeck / pixelio.de

More available books at **www.hansebooks.com**

BONNIE JEAN.

BONNIE JEAN,

A Collection of Papers and Poems relating to the Wife of

ROBERT BURNS.

COMPILED BY

JOHN D. ROSS, LL. D.,

AUTHOR OF "SCOTTISH POETS IN AMERICA,"
EDITOR OF "HIGHLAND MARY," "ROUND BURNS' GRAVE,"
"BURNSIANA," "BURNS' CLARINDA," ETC.

WITH A PREFACE BY

PETER ROSS, LL.D.

AUTHOR OF "THE SCOT IN AMERICA," "A LIFE OF SAINT ANDREW,"
"SCOTLAND AND THE SCOTS," ETC.

" To her memory peace !
With thee she lieth iu gray Dumfries ;—
Hers were thy sorrows, successes, joys ;
She cuddled thy lassies and reared thy boys ;
She dropped o'er thy grave her quick hot tears ;
And gave to thy memory her widow'd years.
REV. ARTHUR JOHN LOCKHART.

NEW YORK :

THE RAEBURN BOOK COMPANY,

1898.

PRESS OF
WALTER W. REID,
NEW YORK.

PREFACE.

I have been requested to write a preface to this volume, this unique tribute to the memory of the wife of Robert Burns, and I comply with pleasure.

So far as I have seen from the proof-sheets, about every event in Jean Armour's life has been chronicled, almost every phase of her character has been considered, by the writers whose contributions make up this interesting book, and so but little remains for me to say. Still I cannot forbear using the opportunity offered to me to lay a stone or two on the cairn which the world has raised, and is still, perhaps unconsciously, raising to the memory of Jean Armour. She was not a woman of genius, she never burned the midnight oil in search of knowledge, nor did she ever wrestle with rhyme, but no one can have studied the life of her husband without acknowledging that it was after her influence over him became supreme, after she was publicly installed as his wife—acknowledged mistress of his heart and hand—that his song attained its highest flights, its most prolific abundance.

Early in what is now a study of Burns' life and works that has extended over more years than were allotted to him who

—moved in manhood as n youth,
Pride of his fellow men,

I formed the idea that the one woman who exerted a real and lasting influence on Burns was her whom in return he has immortalized as Bonnie Jean. All that I have since read has tended to confirm that idea and to make it, to me at least, pass from an idea into a theory, and from a theory into a fact. I am aware, of course, that when people speak of the loves of Burns they think on other women than her who became his wife. Some turn to the hapless Clarinda—one of the most pathetic figures, whatever way we regard her, which the whole course of Scottish literature has given to us; but he was under her influence for only a brief spell—although there is no doubt that her heart was his until the end of her career. Others, and in fact the great majority, turn their thoughts to the cherished figure of Highland Mary, surrounded as it is with romance, love, pathos and mystery. But in spite of all its poetry, its mystery, its depth of romance, and its opportunities for discussion, we turn from Highland Mary to the real heroine of Burns' life, the heroine but for whom Highland Mary would have been no more to the poet after the fit passed than was "Handsome Nell;" the heroine who so elevated and purified his ideas of true womanhood as to make him rise to the sublimity of "To Mary in Heaven;" the wife of his heart, the fixed star of his affections—Jean Armour.

Burns became acquainted with Jean soon after settling in Mossgiel, and the acquaintanceship quickly ripened into mutual love. In all the episodes of Highland Mary, Clarinda and the others, Burns never forgot Jean. He strove to forget her in Edinburgh, but could not efface this woman from his heart. Amid all the glitter of Auld Reekie, in the high tide of his fame, Burns wrote "I feel a miserable blank in my heart for the want of her." When he returned to Ayrshire after the glory of Edinburgh had passed, he was once more at her side. His fame had preceded him; he was no longer the ne'er-do-well he formerly was and old Armour looked on Burns with different eyes. He was now perfectly willing for the union between the poet and his daughter which he had formerly so bitterly opposed; he even urged it. Burns was so disgusted at the servility shown in the change, that he now hung back. But this did not last long, and in August, 1788, Jean and Burns were married, and then set out on the journey of life together, in a little, a very little, home at Mauchline. Thanks to her, Burns' home life was a happy one. We read of no bickerings or upbraidings between husband and wife—none even of those "tiffs" which are supposed to be incidental to the marriage relationship. To him she proved a real, loving help mate. She was passively blind to all his short-comings. She fully appreciated his genius, and understood his temperament better than any one else. She with her evident tact knew how to remove care from his brow and meet his wayward humors with a pretty smile or a cheery song.

As a life partner no one was better suited to get along with the whims and shortcomings of the poet. She made for him a happy home—as happy as she could, and bore up bravely under her sorrows when she saw the crisis of her life at hand and the certainty of widowhood faced her. She was a true woman, a good wife, an affectionate mother, and her memory deserves to receive more of the praise so generously lavished on some of the other loves of the poet than it has yet received.

He immortalized her in many of his songs; he wove a laurel wreath around her as beautiful and endearing, if not as tragic, as that which he wove

around Highland Mary. But there was one difference that speaks volumes for Jean's supremacy in his
. heart. While he sang of her she was before him
with all the faults, frailties and shortcomings of humanity, all the tedium, as it has been called, of
ordinary daily life; while the other had passed
through the veil and so become idealized long before
the " lingering star " aroused in him such a force of
agonized thought, and in time impelled the world, as
a result of his burning words, to elevate the Highland lass into one of the heroines of poetry.

During her married life with Burns, not a whisper
against Jean's wifely character was raised, and during her long widowhood not even the clatter of
Dumfries could cast a slur or suggest a hint to her
detriment. She survived her husband some thirty-
eight years, dying March 26, 1834.

Left as she was in a most helpless condition, the
people of Scotland came to her aid, and soon placed
her beyond the fear of all want, and later made her,
from her standpoint, in easy circumstances. She
seemed to consider from that time that she lived to
guard the fame of her husband. She refused to
leave the little abode in which he died. She kept it
as a show house to such of his admirers as visited
Dumfries, and devoted herself, heart and soul, to

the training of their children. How nobly she succeeded is well known. Some were taken from her
in early life and laid to rest beside their father, but
she was permitted to see others make their way to
honorable positions in the world, while as the sunset
began to fall she found herself the almost sainted
centre of her children's children.

She gave of her means liberally in charity. The
attentions she received, from high and low, never
affected her native good sense, and her home was a
picture of content. She showed in the highest degree that quality of common sense, blended with
kindness, which has done so much to mould the
Scottish character, to shape the Scottish National
life, and if we were to write her epitaph we would
simply sum up her life virtues and failings with the
words; "A good and true woman."

This little volume will doubtless prove acceptable
to the lovers of Scotia's immortal bard everywhere,
and be regarded as a companion work to those in
which the same editor has with loving and discriminating care gathered together a mine of information regarding Highland Mary and Clarinda. It is
from such volumes, dealing with special portions of
the bard's career, or bringing to us a full knowledge
of those who in one way or other shaped that

career, that we gain many valuable side-lights on his own biography, that makes us understand all the more clearly the quality of the gift of gifts which Scotland received when, in 1859,

> "—— a blast o' Jan'war' win'
> Blew hansel in on Robin."

It is hoped this book will meet with a success equal to that at least bestowed on its companion volumes. I am as ready as any one to render homage to the memory of Clarinda, I am ready for the sake of the poetry bearing her name to reverence the heroine we know as Highland Mary. I feel all the interest of a Burns student in Allison Begbie, and love to follow the fortunes of such good and true women as her whose "bonnie e'en" still sparkle in the poet's pages, but Clarinda, Highland Mary, and all the rest, to an admirer of Burns, must yield the foremost place to Bonnie Jean.

PETER ROSS.

New York, October, 1897.

CONTENTS.

BONNIE JEAN.

By J. M. Murdoch, Ayr.

AMONGST all the names in Burns' literature, no
one is so dear to us as "Bonnie Jean." As we
read the variegated career of the greatest Scotsman
ever born, we are dazzled by the splendour of his
versatility, as we are well-nigh moved to tears by
his frailties, we never for a single moment forget his
Bonnie Jean. Jean Armour's fame can never perish. As Burns is borne on the wave of popularity
his Jean will be near him, and Scotsmen all the wide
world o'er will stand on the shore and observe the
two, not with feelings of deep regret and bitter remorse, but with admiration—deep, fervent, and
sincere. No lifeboat will be necessary to rescue the
couple from the grave of some other singers and
heroes; no rockets will be fired to warn admirers of
impending doom, and no funeral service will be held
to say a few parting words regarding their trans-
formation. The printing press has not reached perfection, nor has the fame of Burns and Jean Armour
reached its maximum. And so long as the printing
press is in existence, and Scotsmen are what they
are, so long will Burns and Bonnie Jean survive.
We are sometimes told by those who, presumably,
have not studied human nature, that Burns, with
some cultured, literary lady—say Clarinda—as help-
meet, would have done better work and more of it !
Oh the folly and the indelicacy of these *might have
beens !* Burns had his weaknesses, so have all; but
had we been placed in his position we should assur-

edly have walked in the same plane. Let us not be too finical in our judgments, and thus emulate the hypocrisy of a Mauchline preaching.

We are not amongst those who incessantly and domineeringly cry out that Burns and his Jean were neglected, yea despised, while in the flesh. Burns was aware of his marvellous, preternatural gifts; he was, with few exceptions, received with the respect due to a truly great man; his poems created a greater *furore* in Scotland than the vapid stuff of the majority of present-day writers; and he was, considering the literary remuneration of the time, handsomely paid.

Jean Armour, like many Scotch country lasses, was not an adept in judging *genius*, and she probably took to Burns, not on account of his literary gifts, but on account of his luring, bewitching, persuasive powers in the art of lovemaking. Isn't it curious, isn't it a subject for our deepest meditation, how this young girl, accustomed to the simplicity of rustic life, ignorant of millinery paraphernalia and the rules of etiquette—or tomfoolery—of the rich, and unread in the classics, was, above all others, the one person in the right place, and who, after her marriage, was alwas spoken of in terms of the highest praise? But for her meeting with Burns, Jean Armour would likely have died unknown; but as the lover, the wife and the widow of our grandest lyric poet, she cannot be ignored.

If Burns is to have a corner in our hearts we must also provide a corner for Bonnie Jean. We are inclined to say that Jean Armour did not become famous until after her husband's death, and when we say so we know we are upon treacherous ground. However, such is the case. The genuine admirers of the poet, and the prying slothful sofa recliners generally endeavoured to see Jean as well as Burns, but they were so busy in scanning the greater star, that the lesser got scant justice.

Since the 21st July, 1796, a sad, sad day for Scotland and the world, a greater calamity to the world than the loss of a British Army in Africa, or the sinking of a score of American ironclads, Jean has gradually risen to her true position amongst the revered ones of the earth, and in 1895, we can say, without the fear of contradiction, that her life is a pattern to the mothers of the civilized globe.

Some time ago, an attempt was made to enhance [*Sic !*] the position of Bonnie Jean, but the assumptions and the insinuations were too lifeless to evoke the sympathy of the Burns world. A feature of the present day is controversies regarding the writings of great minds, and whenever writers in the daily or weekly press, or speakers on the platform begin to consider disputed points, one knows that the book, or passage of book, handled is or has been read. This remark is specially applicable to the Bible and Burns. There are thousands of ambitious young men and women yearning for the day when the offspring of their brains shall demand a few letters to the editor, and a discussion at the literary society. But there are contributions and contributions, and many are often times out of place. The article to which we have already referred was like a dead dog on the table of a London or New York drawing-room— nauseous, vomit-creating, and altogether distasteful. A gentleman, animated by a desire for justice, asked "lovers of Burns to rescue noble Jean Armour from the obscurity into which she has been relegated by believers in an idealized Highland Mary." It is out of the question to make Jean Armour stand better in our eyes by a few daubs, out of the pot of vilification, on the memory of Gavin Hamilton's maid-servant. The attachment between Burns and Mary Campbell was artistic in its sincerity; pathetic in its shortness; and this is said after allowing a table-spoonful of salt for poetic license. Mary Campbell is to us what she was to Burns, a true sample of rustic virtue and simplicity, and had the *fiat* of Al-mighty God been sooner directed against Jean Armour than Mary Campbell, the latter would no doubt have been as devoted as the former; but to say that the poet's wife has suffered by the appear-ance of Mary Campbell is a pure surmise, and the outcome of a quasi-Stevensonian brain. The poet was an ordinary mortal, but his characters are not to be found in every man you meet in Fleet Street or Broadway; and in purely love affairs he was the strangest and most wayward son of Adam that ever trod the soil. Woman was to him what the Yankee girl is to Max O'Rell—a person whose path should be strewn with roses, and if the poet in his married state often remembered his Highland Mary, and spoke with candour regarding her, what man or wo-man would deny that he was only thoroughly human? The infinite pathos, the extraordinary superstition, the sublime faith, are all entwined around that inci-dent on the banks of the Ayrshire stream, and no won-der that the darling Son of Scottish Poesy gave vent to his feelings in such matchless verse. Mary Camp-bell's name will ever be cherished with the fondest affection, but never shall we say that it is to us more precious than that of Jean Armour. It is too late in the day to blast the bright halo of romance which surrounds the memory of Highland Mary, and to impugn the poet's candour in connection with that pathetic episode in his phenomenally amorous career. One who looks at events with the spectacles of a historian will not be compelled to grope through darkness to ascertain the unmistakable reliability of the poet concerning his passion for Mary Campbell, and his temporary anguish at the attitude of Jean and her responsible guardians.

Jean Armour's first interview with the poet was of an amusing nature. She was engaged hanging clothes which had been newly washed, and Burns, accompanied by his dog, chanced to pass the green. The member of the canine race with a disregard of the labours of the girl ventured to walk on the linen, with the result that Jean shied a missle of some kind at the offending animal, and the liklihood is she missed, the female arm not being made for such sport. The dog's misdemeanour enabled the two to engage in conversation, and before they parted they were what we in Scotland term "speak acquaint." This incident is only another illustration of what an accident may bring forth. If any dog justified its existence that one did. The whole incident is worthy the brush of some artist, and we are confident Burns' students would be pleased to possess copies. The subsequent disregard of the proprieties and the vicissitudes of the couple are saddening in the extreme; but it is sheer folly to be indignant, as urban Scotland is to-day familiar with hundreds of similiar cases. Burns was not solely to blame for the unfortunate position in which Jean Armour was placed. The parents of Jean became incensed at both; and the one lover dodging the representatives of the law and the other banished from the parental roof, is a picture which must appeal to the sympathies of mankind—a picture dismal in its reality, and without a glimmer of sunshine to dispel the awful gloom. But the sun did not always remain behind the clouds. Genius, or abilities, or graces of any kind, should not be taken into account in deciding questions of State, Church, or Law, and we fancy Burns would have been the last person in the world to have differed from such a dictum. But there are many to-day who will say a person of the mental grandeur of Burns should have been treated with more consideration. Not at all; his faults were of his own making, and the law makes no distinction of persons. There is this point in Burns' favour, that he never would have given Jean the cold shoulder, time alone being all that was necessary to put matters right. Jean's father was not overstepping the bounds of propriety in taking out a warrant, but we think that in a moment of wrath, and when their pride felt the sting, the parents treated Jean somewhat harshly. The acclamation of a discerning public healed the sore, although the inconsistency of Jean's father is apt to make us grin. Even in an estimate of Bonnie Jean a subject like the above cannot be omitted. The vicissitudes must have had an effect upon the after career of Jean. All through these troubles she bore up bravely, quietly, and lovingly. The alliance was creditable to Burns. That it was highly expedient cannot be doubted. Morality has its codes, and poor, unfortunate Burns did not allow his compeers to cavil at his preaching. Altogether the poet is picturesque here. It is appropriate to introduce at this stage one or two of the poet's references to his wife.

To Miss Peggy Chalmers he wrote:—

" I have married my Jean. I had a long and much-loved fellow creature's happiness or misery in my determination, and I durst not trifle with so important a deposit; nor have I any cause to repent it. If I have not got polite tittle-tattle, modish manners, and fashionable address, I am not sickened and disquieted with the multiform curse of boarding-school affectation; and I have got the handsomest figure, the sweetest temper, the soundest constitution, and the kindest heart in the country."

To Mrs. Dunlop (his valued correspondent), he said in a letter:—"Your surmise, madam, is just; I am indeed a husband. The most placid good nature and sweetness of disposition; a warm heart, gratefully devoted with all its powers to love me; vigorous health and sprightly cheerfulness, set off to the best advantage by a more than commonly handsome figure; these, I think, in a woman, may make a good wife, though she should never have read a page but the Scriptures of the Old and New Testaments, nor have danced in a brighter assembly than a penny pay-wedding."

And of the poet himself Jean said, in a conversation with Hew Ainslie, "He was never fractious—aye gude-natured and kind baith to the bairns and to me." All the facts obtainable as to the life of the couple go to show that Jean on no occasion proved a traitor. Throughout the eight years of light and darkness, when there was a variety of circumstances sufficient to cool the ardour of most lovers, the two understood each other to a nicety. There is one incident which will ever redound to the credit of Bonnie Jean. In itself it is the highest monument in favour of her prudence and the intensity of her love. The daughter of the poet, born in March, 1791, was brought home to the house of Burns, and taken charge of by Mrs. Burns. The child was soon after found by Jean's father in the same cradle with a babe of her own, and, in order to keep down din, she replied to her father that the second baby was one of whom she was taking temporary charge for a sick friend. Jean brought up the child to womanhood, always putting it on an equality with her own offspring. We don't think it is too much to say that one woman out of three would have failed, and failed miserably, in Jean Armour's position. Our remark places a reflection upon the mammoth genius whom Jean adored and served with a fidelity seldom exhibited in the pages of romance and history; but when we take into account that the stream of poesy was often kept back by the sluices of adversity, misfortune, and occasional bacchanalian enjoyments, we cannot, if we are to display the undisguised truth, come to any other conclusion. Spite of the opportunities for display of the old Adam, Jean Armour adopted the attitude of a trained diplomat. We shall mainly attribute her success to her homeliness, amiability, sound common sense, and long-suffering.

When we sometimes stroll past Alloway Kirkyard, an incident full of the richest pathos, generally crosses our mind. The incident displays the heroism of Bonnie Jean. In the Spring after Burns died, two men, passing through Dumfries, visited St. Michael's Churchyard. Being strangers, they did not know where Burns' remains lay. They observed a female in deep mourning, sitting on the ground, and one of them addressed her as follows:—"Mistress, we are strangers, and we would feel obliged if you could show us the grave of Burns." Pointing to the mound at her feet, and bursting into tears, she answered, "That is his grave, and I am his widow." The two men apologized for their intrusion, tendered their heartfelt condolence, and left the spot to study the picture. Had the spirit of the bard been hovering around the spot, wouldn't there have been cause for thankfulness at the attitude of Jean? The world was not the same to her since her dearest friend was not of it; the poetry of cold type was not the poetry of the human being.

Before we close this paper we shall give an account of another incident, equally reliable. One beautiful Saturday in the Autumn of 1893, we were standing on the auld brig o' Doon. A fierce noon-day sun caused visitors to seek the sylvan shade, the trouts ever and anon jumped out of the water, the larks rendered a pæan of praise, the trees and the flowers sent forth their sweetest perfume, and the whirr of the reaping machine spoke of the goodness of the Wise Providence who rules over us.

On the road was an aged figure—a pilgrim at the shrine of Robin. He was talkative—he came from America. "I have," he said, "long wished to see the auld clay biggin, and the banks and braes o' Bonnie Doon; to-day I have seen them, and shall go home to die in peace." Unquestionably noble words. They inform us of what the poet did for humanity. Not Jean alone, but all mankind mourned his loss; and this American wanderer, perhaps living near the Alleghany ranges, could not think he had done his duty on earth without crossing the wide Atlantic to pay his devotions at the shrine of Burns. There is a religion in the two incidents more deep and more vital than that of the bellicose Christians who parade their sanctity.

We hold Jean's name in honour because she heroically and cheerfully did her part as the wife of Burns; and moreover, did she not, throughout the thirty-eight years of her widowhood—she was but twenty-three years of age when she married—defend the poet's name and fame when numerous attacks were made by unscrupulous critics and nonentities? The Doon and the Ayr, whose praises are chanted in every corner of the habitable globe—in the *de-*

mesnes of the rich, and in the cotters' houses and log cabins of the poor—are as classical as the Nile and the Ganges; Mauchline, Tarbolton, and Alloway, are as famous as Jerusalem, Bethlehem, and Jericho; but the rushing waters of sentiment, although they sometimes benumb the tongue and stay the pen, shall not prevent us from laying this wreath upon the grave of Bonnie Jean.

BONNIE JEAN.

By James Gillan.

A picture hangs upon the wall
Of this dim city home of mine,
And ofttimes as my glances fall
Upon its face it seems to shine,
And smile as in the days gone bye,
When Cupid drew aside the screen
That hid from his enraptured eye
The beaming face of Bonnie Jean.

The colour mantles on the brow
O'er which the raven love locks play
The swarthy face once more aglow
Beams like a sunny day in May.
And in the jet black eyes again
The tender light of love is seen
And from the lips a dulcet strain
Keeps murmuring of Bonnie Jean.

A cloud across the forehead creeps,
A darker flash in the eyes
As some stern thought unbridled sweeps—
Or memories of base deeds arise
To fill his human heart with ire
And raise an anger swift and keen,
Yet still the lips like some sweet lyre
Keep murmuring of Bonnie Jean.

I see him in my fancy rove
Through smiling meadows—round the hills.
I hear his laughter in the grove,
I hear his music by the rills

That tarried in their winding flight
Beneath the silv'ry moon at 'een
While he sang to the starry night
The praises of his Bonnie Jean.

He tuned all tender strings that lie
Beneath the keyboard of the heart
From music scrolls that filled the sky.
And poesy held the leaves apart
While he sang loud, for coming days
A song more sweet than e'er had been
Sent up from mortal heart in praise
Of Scotland and his Bonnie Jean.

·I do not deem my cottage poor,
This picture is a richer gem
Than any glittering Kohenoor
Upon a princely diadem,
And like a star it points the way
By Scotia's choral pastimes green
Where sweetest memories may stray
With Robbie and his Bonnie Jean.

BONNIE JEAN.

By Dr. Robert Chambers.

From "The Life and Writings of Robert Burns."

*** In the first of these versicles, he alludes to the attachment which he had found for the most celebrated of all his heroines, and his subsequent wife, JEAN. She was the daughter of a master-mason named Armour, residing in the village of Mauchline. Her husband has perfectly described her at this period of her life—

> 'A dancin', sweet, young handsome quean,
> Of guileless heart !'

The acquaintance seems to have commenced not long after the poet took up his residence at Mossgiel. There was a race at Mauchline in the end of April, and there it was customary for the young men, with little ceremony, to invite such girls as they liked off the street into a humble dancing-hall, where a fiddler had taken up his station to give them music. The payment of a penny for a dance was held by the minstrel as guerdon sufficient. Burns and Jean happened to be in the same dance, but not as partners, when some confusion and a little merriment was excited by his dog tracking his footsteps through the room. He playfully remarked to his partner that ' he wished he could get any of the lassies to like him as well as his dog did.' A short while after, he passed through the Mauchline washing-green, where Jean, who had overheard his remark, was bleaching clothes. His dog running over the clothes, the young maiden desired him to call it off, and this led them into conversation.

Archly referring to what passed at the dance, she asked him if 'he had yet got any of the lassies to like him as well as his dog?' From that time their intimacy commenced. The affections of Burns were quickly centred upon her. There were other maidens in Mauchline, some with weightier attractions, but no one could henceforth compete with Jean. So he himself tells us:—

> In Mauchline there dwells six proper young belles,
>   The pride of the place and its neighborhood a',
> Their carriage and dress a stranger would guess,
>   In Lon'on or Paris, they'd gotten it a'.
> Miss Miller is fine, Miss Markland's divine,
>   Miss Smith she has wit and Miss Betty is braw,
> There's beauty and fortune to get wi' Miss Morton ;
>   But Armour's the Jewel for me o' them a'.

*   *   *   *

The commencement of Burns' acquaintance with his Jean has already been touched upon. This young woman had now been for upwards of a year the goddess of his idolatry. He had, rather oddly, written no songs which can be certainly traced as in her honour; but he had expressed his admiration of her in his *Epistle to Davie*, in the *Address to The Deil*, and *The Vision*. When it appeared in the Spring of 1786, that love had become transgression, Burns and brother were beginning to fear that their farm would prove a ruinous concern. He yielded, nevertheless, to the wish of his unhappy partner to acknowledge her as his wife, and thus repair as far as possible the consequences of their error. He gave her such an acknowledgment in writing, a document sufficient in the law of Scotland to constitute what is called an irregular, though perfectly valid, marriage. Jean probably expected that, if her parents were first made acquainted with her fault by the announcement of clandestine nuptials, they would look more mildly upon it; for such is a common course of circumstances in her rank of life in Scotland. But it was otherwise in this case. Knowing well that Burns was not in flourishing circumstances it appeared to the father that marriage, so far from mending the matter, made it worse. Burns came forth on this occasion with all the manliness which his character would have led us to expect. He admitted the hopelessness of his present circumstances; but he offered to go out to Jamaica in the hope of bettering them, and of coming home in a few years and claiming Jean as his wife. If this plan should not meet Mr. Armour's approbation, he was willing to descend even to the condition of a common labourer, in order to furnish means for the present support of his wife and her expected offspring. It does not seem to have been one of his hopes that the wondrous poems lying in the table-drawer at Mossgiel could help in aught to lighten the burden he was willing to incur. Mr. Armour met every proposal with rejection. The course he took will only be intelligible if we reflect that in Scottish village there is little of the delicacy as to female purity which prevails in more refined circles. Armour reflected that his daughter, if free from her connections with the ill-starred poet, might yet hope for a comfortable settlement in life. He therefore announced his resolution, if possible to annul the marriage, such as it was. Yielding to his demand, probably preferred in no mild mood, Jean surrendered the paper to her angry father. There were some violent and distressing scenes between the parties. Not endowed by nature with very deep or abiding feelings, and depressed in spirit by the sense of her error, Jean, to the utter confusion of Burns, appeared less willing to cleave to her husband than to her father. The poet viewed her conduct with deep resentment, and was thrown by it into a state of mind, which, according to his own confession, 'had very nearly given him one or two of the principal qualifications for a place among those who have lost the chart and mistaken the reckoning of rationality.' He instantly made up his mind to exile from his much-beloved country. His poverty and imprudence made that course desirable, and, after the mortification he had met with, he had no longer the wish to stay at home. He therefore agreed with a Dr. Douglas to go out to Jamaica as a book-keeper on his estate. To raise money for his passage, Mr. Hamilton advised him to publish his poems by subscription, believing that his name had already secured him a sufficient number of friends to make the sale of a small volume certain, and to a moderate extend profitable. We have seen, from many expressions in the poems of the past writer, that Burns was in a state of mind regarding them to make this plan highly acceptable to him. Accordingly, without any loss of time, proposals or subscription papers were thrown off and circulated amongst the friends of the unfortunate bard.

*　　　*　　　*　　　*

Though he had been effectually separated, or, it might be said divorced from Jean Armour, and was much incensed by her conduct and that of her relatives, he had never been able to detach her from his heart. Gusts of passion for different individuals had passed through his bosom, even while resting in what he called ' the Greenland bay of difference' in Edinburgh; but still the image of the simple Mauchline girl resided at the core, and would not quit its place. On now returning to his rustic retreat, and

accidentally meeting her, his ancient flames were revived, and he was welcomed to her father's house.
In a short time the pair became as intimate as ever.

*　　　*　　　*　　　*

The bachelor life of Burns was now drawing to a
close. His new home proved wholly unready for
the reception of his wife, he had obtained temporary
accomodation for her at a neighboring farm. Accordingly, in the first week of December (1788) he
conducted Mrs. Burns to the banks of the Nith.
During the preceeding week two servant-lads and a
servant-girl had migrated thither from Mauchline,
with some cart-loads of the plenishing made by Mor-
rison; besides, I presume, a handsome four-posted
bed, which Mrs. Dunlop had contributed as her marriage gift. The servant-lass, named Elizabeth
Smith, still lives at Irvine [1851]. She reports that
Mrs. Burns was anxious, on going into a district
where she was wholly a stranger, to obtain the services of a young woman whom she already knew.
Elizabeth was engaged accordingly, but not till her
father, in his anxiety for her moral wellfare, had
exacted a formal promise from Burns to keep a strict
watch over her conduct, and, in particular, to exercise her duly in the Catechism, in both of which
points she admits he was most faithful to his promise. About a mile below Ellisland there is a small
tract of ground which has once been encircled by the
waters of the Nith, partly through natural channels
and partly through an artificial trench. Here rises
an old dismantled tower, with more modern buildings adjoining to it on two of its sides—the whole
forming the farm-buildings of *The Isle ;* for such is
the name of the place, still remained, although one
of the ancient water courses is now only a rusty

piece of ground. The place, which has an antiquated, and even somewhat romantic appearance, was the property of Mr. Newell, writer in Dumfries, whose family had lived in it during the Summer, but only for a short time, in consequence of certain nocturnal sounds in the old tower having led to a belief that it was haunted. What added a little, or perhaps not a little to the *eeriness* of the spot, was that the old burying-ground of Dunscore, containing the sepulchre of the dreaded persecutor, Grierson, of Lagg, was in the immediate neighbourhood. Such was the 'moated grange,' at which the illustrious poet welcomed home the mistress of his heart—the fascinating, never to be forgotten, Jean Armour. We may well believe that it was a time of great happiness to Burns when he first saw his mistress installed in her little mansion, and felt himself the master of the household, however humble—looked up to by a wife as 'the goodman' and by a host of dependants as 'the master.' Who can refrain from sympathizing with the great ill-requited poet in this brief exception from a painful life.

BONNIE JEAN.

By Robert Burns Begg.

Re-printed from the Burns Chronicle, No. 1, by permission of the author.

Jean Armour was born in February 1767, at Mauchline, Ayrshire, where her father James Armour was a respectable master-mason or contractor, in good employment and enjoying the confidence and esteem of the district in which he was located, He appears to have been exemplary in his life but like many worthy men he was somewhat rigid and austere in his disposition and belonged to the stricter sect of Religionists called the "Auld Lichts." Mrs. Armour seems to have been an affectionate and devoted wife and mother, but her mental bias differed from that of her husband, and appears to have partaken somewhat of the gay and frivolous. They had a family of eleven children, whom they reared and maintained creditably and comfortably; for Mr. Armour, in addition to the income derived from his trade, was proprietor of house property of some value in the village. His daughter, Jean, was a bright sprightly and affectionate girl, and she was naturally adored by her parents—her father especially being intensely proud of her. On her part, she seems to have had a deep regard and veneration for her father, as is evidenced by the fact that she, at the most trying crisis of a young girl's life, was ready at his command to sacrifice the dearest and tenderest aspirations of her nature.

Her childhood was spent at Mauchline amid the usual associations surrounding Scottish village life, and when Burns, (then in his 26th year) along with his widowed mother and his brothers and sisters, came to reside at Mossgiel, within a mile from Manchline, she had barely emerged from her "teens." From the description of her handed down to us by those who knew her at this interesting period of her life, we gather that she was a remarkably sweet and attractive brunette of a bright affectionate nature, gifted with an attractive smiling face, lighted up by a pair of very bewitching dark eyes. Her person was well formed and firmly knit and her movements were at all times graceful and easy. In manner she was frank and unaffected and she was kindly and winning in her disposition.

Her first meeting with Burns did not occur until sometime after the Burns family settled at Mossgiel, in March, 1784. The meeting was a casual one, at a rustic dance in Mauchline on the evening of the village races. On that occassion she does not appear to have had any direct intercourse with her future husband, but she seems to have treasured up in her heart an observation which she overheard him making in his usual frank jocular style. During one of the dances, some confusion and merriment was occasioned by Burns' collie persisting in tracking its master's footsteps and on Burns' attention being drawn to his intrusive follower, he said : "I wish I could find a lassie as fond of me as my dog." Very shortly after the evening of the dance, Jean was one day engaged bleaching linen on the village green of Mauchline, when Burns passed accompanied as usual by his faithful collie. The dog in its frisky frolics intruded itsself among the cloth Jean was spreading on the grass, and she besought Burns to recall the animal to his side. Having complied with her request, Burns naturally lingered to exchange observations with her, and her frank remark—"Have you found any lassie yet to love ye as well as yer dog"— accompanied, as it no doubt was, by a fascinating archness of expression, must have gone straight to the Poet's highly impressionable heart. With two such natures an acquaintanceship thus begun on a key-note so suggestive, could lead to only one result —an immediate attraction to each other, by the tenderest and most overpowering predilection which sways the human heart.

Opportunities for the lovers meeting were not infrequent, for Burns' favorite "howff" during his leisure hours, was the Whiteford Arms—an inn so closely adjoining the Armours' house, that confidences could easily be interchanged at pleasure from one of the back windows of the inn, which looked into one of the windows of Jean's house behind. A close and tender intimacy thus became established, and it was maintained for upwards of a year, by meetings as frequent as Burns' occupation on his farm rendered possible. Unfortunately, these interviews had to be conducted with the utmost secrecy, for both lovers well knew that old Mr. Armour's bitterest prejudices would be opposed to the idea of Burns as his son-in-law. This intercourse naturally led to Burns becoming attached to Jean by a love as ardent, permanent and sincere, as even his deep emotional nature was capable of feeling. We find this passion, in its earliest stages, finding expression in such versicles as *The Mauchline Belles* and *The Mauchline Lady*, until it gradually acquires a deeper and more earnest tone, and culminates at length in the fervid impassioned appeal on Jean's behalf, introduced into the admirable epistle to David Sillar :

" O, all ye Pow'rs who rule above !
O Thou whose very self art love !
Thou know'st my word sincere
The life blood streaming thro' my heart,
Or my more dear Immortal part
Is not more fondly dear !
When heart carroding care and grief
Deprive my soul of rest,
Her dear idea brings relief,
And solace to my breast.
Thou being all-seeing,
O hear my fervent pray'r !
Still take her, and make her,
Thy most peculiar care !"

Was ever weak woman thus wo'ed—and who can
wonder if the simple hearted village maiden, in all
the loving trust of her affectionate and confiding
nature, blindly surrendered herself to a lover so
impassioned, and who could woo so effectively ?

" Who made the heart, 'tis He alone
Decidedly can try us,
He knows each chord its varying tone,
Each spring its various bias :
Then at the balance let's be mute,
We never can adjust it ;
What's done we partly may compute.
But know not what's resisted."

At length the time arrived when concealment of
their tender intercourse was no longer possible, and
in the Spring of 1786, Burns and Jean signed a
formal acknowledgement of marriage, and thus become legally, although informally, husband and wife.
This declaration was signed openly and was en-
trusted to the custody of Mr. Robert Aitken, Writer,
Ayr, a mutual friend both of Burns and of the
Armours. The biographers of the Poet, following
Lockhart, look upon this natural proceeding on

Burns' part as an act of mere justice and necessity, rather than as a purely voluntary one. It is dfficult to see why it should be so regarded. His affection for Jean was deep, permanent and sincere, and in every way it differed widely from the erratic and ephemeral attachments he was so prone to form. From the earliest period of their acquaintance he seems to have been drawn towards her by a strong community of feeling, and it is clear that from the first, he appropriated her as peculiarly "his own" in the tenderest sense of the phrase. The hopes which he centred in her were not the mere ardent aspirations of the moment, but a fond and persistent clinging to the happy prospect of life-long and loving companionship with her in the placid haven of domestic life. She was undoubtedly his beau ideal of a wife, suited in every sense to his nature and disposition and eminently fitted in a practical way, for the line of life he had adopted at the time their intimacy began. In a letter which he sometime afterwards wrote to Mrs. Dunlop of Dunlop, he thus expresses his estimate of Jean's suitability as a wife: —"The most placid good nature and sweetness of disposition, a warm heart gratefully devoted with all its powers to love me, vigorous health, and sprightly cheerfulness, set off to the best advantage by a more than common handsome figure—these I think in a woman may make a good wife though she should not have read a page but the Scriptures of the Old and New Testament, nor have danced in brighter assembly than a penny pay wedding."

In the early stages of their intimacy no immediate views of marriage could be entertained by either of them, and at the best their union must have been a remote, although not the less, a very real, as well as a very happy, prospect. His family had then newly

entered on their tenancy of Mossgiel farm with their
means sorely crippled by recent losses at Lochlea,
and as month after month sped over the heads of
the happy lovers, drawing the tender tie between
them still closer and closer, their prospect of
marriage became more and more remote. Mossgiel
farm had failed to yield the return anticipated and
by the time the declaration of marriage was signed,
Burns had actually formed the resolution to leave
his native land and seek for better fortune in
Jamaica, and it was fondly hoped that the private
marriage would be regarded not only in the light of
a reparation to the Armours, for the distress entailed
upon them, but that it might also secure for Jean
the shelter of her father's roof until Burns had provided for her a home in the country of his adoption.

In their plans thus anxiously and lovingly laid,
the unfortunate pair failed to take into account the
unyielding prejudice of old Mr. Armour. The intelligence of his daughter's unfortunate condition
was to him a terrible humiliation, and he is said to
have swooned away under the blow, and far from
the attempted reparation lessening his displeasure it
only intensified his opposition to such an extent, that
rather than entertain the prospect of Burns ever
claiming his daughter as his wife, he induced Mr.
Aitken, the custodier of the declaration of marriage,
to cancel the signatures attached to that document.
There is no doubt, that Jean, in her utter wretched-
ness, was induced by filial love and obedience, to
acquiesce in her parent's harsh and unjust proceeding and she was at once sent off to Paisley, to live
with her uncle there, so as to be beyond the reach of
Burns' seductive influence. The misery she must
have endured during her temporary retirement at
Paisley, no one can ever estimate. Severed from

him she had loved and still loved so fondly and blindly, and severed too by a harshness and injustice to which she had actually although unwillingly been a party—discarded in a sense by the parents she revered so highly, and intruded into the house of relatives, who, at the best, must have regarded her presence among them in the light of a painful necessity—her thoughts must have been little calculated to impart either comfort or hopefulness to the prospect that lay before her.

To Burns, too, the rupture must have brought an intolerable load of misery. He was naturally deeply incensed at the treatment he had experienced at the hands of Jean's parents, and he was cut to the heart at Jean's "perfidy," as he styled it, in allowing herself to be induced to repudiate her obligations as his wife. He thus expresses his feelings on this painful occasion in a letter to his friend, John Ballantyne, Ayr, "would you believe it though I had not a hope nor a wish to make her mine after her conduct, yet when he [Aitken], told me the names were cut out of the paper, my heart died within me—he cut my heart with the news." This certainly is not the language of a man who has been released from an unkindly and lifelong bond, in which he had involuntarily entangled himself from a mere sense of justice.

It is true, that in some of his more rollicking letters to his boon companions and more intimate associates, he attempts in a spirit of bravado to make light of the calamity which had befallen him, but the attempt is a poor one at the best, and every now and then expressions escape him which disclose only too painfully the utter desolation of heart which Jean's unlooked for desertion had entailed upon him. No student of Burns' life and character would dream

of taking him *au serieux* in letter of the nature referred to, but would rather prefer to gather his real
sentiments from the language he employs in addressing his more staid and serious correspondents, such
as Dr. Moore, whom in the Summer recess of 1787,
he thus writes:—"It was a shocking affair which I
cannot yet bear to recollect and it had very nearly
given me one or two of the principal qualifications
for a place among those who have lost the chart and
mistaken the reckoning of rationality." In writing
also to Dr. Arnot, of Dalquhatswood, about the same
period, he says, "How I bore this, can only be conceived, all powers of recital labour far far behind.
There is a pretty large portion of bedlam in the composition of a poet at any time, but on this occasion I
was nine parts and nine-tenths out of ten stark star-
ing mad."

His allusions to this painful theme in his poetic
effusions of this period are also crouched in a fervour
and sincerity of expression which leaves no doubt of
the depth and permanency of his unhappiness. We
find pointed pathetic suggestions of it in his sonnet
composed on Spring and in the most exquisite of all
his poems—his address to a mountain daisy. We
find it too expressed in plainer and more pointed
language in his "Ode to Ruin."

> "With stern resolved despairing eye,
>   I see each aiméd dart,
> For one has cut my dearest tie,
>   And quivers in my heart.
> Then lowering and pouring,
>   The storm no more I dread :
> Though thick'ning and black'ning
>   Round my devoted head."

But the most expressive of all, is his reference to

the subject to be found in "The Lament" which he composed to this occasion.

> "The plighted faith, the mutual flame,
>   The oft protested Powers above,
> The promised father's tender name :
>   These were the pledges of my love."

> "Ye wingéd hours that o'er us passed,
>   Enraptured more the more enjoyed,
> Your dear remembrance in my breast,
>   My fondly treasured thoughts employed,
> That breast how dreary now and void,
>   For her too scanty once of room,
> Even every ray of hope destroy'd,
>   And not a wish to glid the gloom."

The rupture seems to have occured early in Spring and Jean did not return from Paisley until July. Actuated by his clinging affection for her, Burns seems to have made an effort to re-establish their intercourse immediately on her return to her father's house, but Mrs. Armour repelled the Poet's overtures with anger and disdain, and even Jean herself, influenced by her parents, seems to have discouraged Burns' well meant and loving advances. Fortunately for Burns, he, unlike poor Jean, had in the midst of these painful experiences many engrossing subjects to distract his thoughts. He had, in the first place, the publication of the first edition of his poems, which he was then engaged in seeing through the press, at Kilmarnock. But his most effectual distraction was his brief but romantic engagement to "Highland Mary" which however fickle and inconsistent it may appear to be, actually occured during the interval which elapsed between Jean's desertion and his departure for Edinburgh, in November. To Burns, *love* was an absolute and clamant necessity, and in his desire to supplant Jean, he could not have selected a more endearing substitute than the sweet dairy-maid at Coilsfield, and the very impetuosity of his solemn matrimonial engagement with Mary Campbell at a time when his circumstances almost precluded the possibility of marriage, only affords proof of the "widowed" condition of his heart.

In September, 1786, Jean, in the house of her parents at Mauchline, gave birth to twins—a boy and girl. Intelligence of the event was at once communicated to Burns at Mossgiel, and arrangements were made for transferring the boy to Mossgiel to be nurtured there, by the Poet's mother and sisters, while the girl remained with its mother at Mauchline. The boy bore his father's name, and in after life he attained to a good position in the Government Civil Service. The girl was named Jean afer her mother, but she died after a brief existence of only fourteen months, and was interred in Mauchline Churchyard. The birth of Jean's children, did not tend to promote a reconciliation with the Armours. On the contrary it seems to have embittered their prejudices more and more, and in order to make the rupture permanent and complete, formal steps were taken *ex facie ecclesiae* to undo whatever legal effect the private marriage might be supposed to have.

These unhappy proceedings seem to have barely terminated when Dr. Blacklock's suggestion that Burns should come to Edinburgh, opened up before him, a new and dazzling prospect, and on 27th November, 1786, he left Mossgiel for Edinburgh, and did not return until June of the year following. In the interval Jean remained in her father's house at Mauchline, striving to find in her novel duty as a mother some little solace for her misery and unhappiness, while Burns, even in the midst of the exciting experiences of his first winter in the Scottish Metropolis, found his thoughts oft reverting to Jean, at Mauchline. Writing to Gavin Hamilton, in the beginning of 1787, he says, " to tell the truth I feel a miserable blank in my heart from the want of her." It is not surprising therefore to find that on his return from Edinburgh, in the following summer, his first thought is "his Jean" and instead of taking up his residence at Mossgiel, he puts up at the Whiteford Arms, and he seems to have remained there for several days, previous to his secret pilgrimage to Argyleshire, to ascertain the particulars of Mary Campbell's sad and untimely death.

His reason for taking up his abode at "Johnnie Dows," must have been his desire to renew his loving intercourse with Jean, and he accordingly called at the Armours' house immediately on his arrival at Mauchline, ostensibly, according to his own statement, simply to see "his daughter" then an infant of barely nine months, but no doubt the child's mother was a still more potent attraction. One can fancy the rapture with which the lovers must have met after their painful and protracted severance. Their mutual affection remained unabated and but for the injudiciousness of Jean's parents, a complete re-union would no doubt have been the immediate result. Burns' proud nature had been sorely wounded by the harsh and disdainful treatment he had received during the previous summer, and his resentment towards Jean's parents was intensified by having super-added to it a feeling of utter contempt for their "mean servility" when he found himself—owing to the change in his worldly prospects—received by them with great civility and with every indication of their desire to promote the union which they had persistently rejected only a few months before.

The contempt which Burns felt at this sudden change of treatment, and the motives from which it sprung was too deep to be easily overcome, and although it does not seem to have interferred in any way with his loving intercourse with Jean, it prevented him from taking immediate steps to secure her happiness by re-instating her in her position as his wife.

Under the influence of this feeling, Burns again returned to Edinburgh for a brief temporary visit, leaving Jean and her child behind him in her father's house at Mauchline After spending sometime in Edinburgh and visiting at Harveston, Ochtertyre, and elsewhere, he returned to Edinburgh in the end of October. By this time it is clear that he had decided on a definite and practical means of livelihood for himself and those dependant upon him, and in accordance therewith, he makes an excursion to Dumfriesshire to inspect the farm of Ellisland, which he contemplated leasing. In combination with his farming project he conceived the idea of securing an appointment in the excise, so as to have "his commission in his pocket for any emergency of fortune."

In this carefully planned and thoroughly sensible scheme there cannot be a doubt that Burns had uppermost in his heart a desire to find a suitable home for his wife and children, and when in the end of January 1788, in the very heart of his laboured love-traffic, with his "divine Clarinda," intelligence is conveyed to him in Edinburgh that poor Jean is once more under a cloud on his account, he acts with a promtitude and practical effect which is clearly indicative of a preconceived and deliberate resolution. At the time he received the intelligence he was dis-

abled by an injury to one of his knees and he was prevented from hastening to Jean's side as he otherwise
would have done. He, however, wrote at once, to
his steadfast friend, William Muir, of Tarbolton
Mill—the veritable Willie of the now famed " Willie's
Mill "—and solicited him and his wife to receive
Jean into their house, until he—as he in nautical
phrase states in a letter to his sea-faring friend
Brown—"can himself take command." In little
more than a fortnight he is on his way to Mossgiel,
and immediately on his arrival he visits Jean in her
retirement, and in his own language "reconciles her
to her mother ; takes a room for her, and takes her
to his arms." After a brief visit to Edinburgh in
the beginning of March, Burns is back in Mauchline
beside his wife, before the end of the month. Ten
days previously Jean had again given birth to twins
—two girls—both of whom died a few days afterwards, and so soon as the state of her health permitted, the reunited lovers went through a simple
and binding formality in the business Chambers of
Gavin Hamilton, Writer, in Mauchline, and Jean
was once more, and openly reinstated in her position
as Burns' wife. This marriage was solemnly confirmed by the Kirk Session of Mauchline, on the 5th
of August, and Burns and his wife took up their
abode temporarily in a house in Mauchline, now
forming the corner house of the street called Back
Causeway overlooking the Churchyard of Mauchline.
Here in a house of two rooms, Jean spent nearly
four months of unalloyed happiness, after two years
of deep mental anguish to both her and her husband.
Happily this was all now at an end, and Burns in
his correspondence at this period, breathes nothing
but deep and fervent self-congratulation on the important step he had taken. In a letter written by

him, three months after the re-union, and addressed to Mrs. Dunlop, of Dunlop, he says in reference to his prospect of finding substantial happiness in his married life : " To jealousy or infidelity I am an equal stranger ; my preservative from the first is the most thorough consciousness of her sentiments of honour, and her attachment to me.. My antidote against the last is my long and deep-rooted affection for her. I can easily fancy a more agreeable companion for my journey through life, but upon my honour I have never seen the individual instance. In household matters, of aptness to learn and activity to execute, she is eminently mistress ; and during my absence in Nithsdale she is regularly and constantly apprenticed to my mother and sisters in their dairy and other rural business."

During the period that Mrs. Burns continued to reside at Mauchline, Burns' time was almost equally divided between that place and Ellisland at the latter of which he was superintending the operations on his farm, and especially the erection of a new dwelling house, for the accommodation of his wife and children. The distance between the two places, was forty-six miles, and as the journey was performed on horseback, Burns often started from Ellisland as early as three in the morning. During this period, his deep and fervent attachment to his wife finds expression in his exquisite song, *O' a' the airts the wind can blaw*, and the powerful effect of this truly powerful love ode, is much enhanced, if it is studied in the light of the loneliness and discomfort which at this time surrounded Burns at Ellisland. He gives a graphic description of his experiences in a letter to Miss Chalmers : " Jean ' my Jean ' is still at Mauchline, and I am building my house, for this hovel that I shelter in, while occasionally here is pervious to every blast that blows, and every shower that falls; and I am preserved from being chilled to death by being suffocated with smoke." In an atmosphere so prosaic and uninspiring, it is pleasant to think of the youthful husband and father, in his loneliness and discomfort, welcoming the breeze as laden with tender messages from that humble home in the west, over which the tenderest feelings of his heart hovered so fondly.

We have too, in connection with this period, one of the only two letters which have been preserved, addressed by Burns to his wife. It is dated 12th September, 1788

"MY DEAR LOVE:
I received your kind letter with a pleasure which no letter but one from you could have given me. I dream of you the whole night long, but alas! I fear it will be three weeks yet ere I can hope for the happiness of seeing you. My harvest is going on; I have some to cut down still but I put in two stacks to-day, so I am as tired as a dog. * * * * I have written my long thought on letter to Mr. Graham, Commissioner of Excise, and have sent a sheet full of poetry besides. Now I talk of poetry, I had a fine strathspey among my hands, to make verses to, for Johnson's collection, which I intend, as my honeymoon song."

The house at Ellisland was not completed at the time expected, although Burns supervised the operations with a zeal and anxiety suggestive more of the ardour of the lover than the mere urgency of the husband and father. His appeal to his joiner, in regard to the delay in the building operations, is unique, and must have formed a genuine novelty in the usual correspondence connected with that worthy tradesman's business:

"Necessity obliges me to go into my new house even before it be plastered. I will inhabit the one end until the other is finished. About three weeks more I think will at farthest be my time beyond which I cannot stay in this present house. If ever you wished to deserve the blessing of him that was ready to perish; if ever you were in a situation that a little kindness would have rescued you from many evils; if ever you hope to find rest in future states of untried being, get these matters of mine ready."

In spite of this fervid appeal the house was not fit for occupancy before winter set in, and Burns was obliged to secure a temporary residence in "the Isle," a romantic spot, situated on the banks of the Nith, about a mile from Ellisland. Here, in the first week of December, 1788, he brought his young wife, preceded by two servant lads and a servant girl, and some cart loads of furniture and other household plenishing. Who can doubt the joy and pride with which Mrs. Burns rejoined her husband in her new home, and his happiness too was, as may easily be imagined, in every sense complete. Two months later, in writing to a correspondent in Edinburgh, he bursts into the following glowing rhapsody, which must be regarded as merely the reflex of the happiness he himself was then experiencing: "Love is the Alpha and Omega of human enjoyment. All the pleasures, all the happiness of my humble compeers flow immediately and directly from this delightful source. It is the spark of celestial fire which lights up the wintry hut of poverty, and makes the cheerful mansion, warm, comfortable, and gay. It is the examination of Divinity, that preserves the sons and daughters of rustic labour from degenerating into the brutes with which they daily hold converse. Without it, life to the poor inmates of the cottage would be a damning gift."

After a brief but happy period of six months spent at "the Isle," possession was at length obtained of their own house at Ellisland, and about three months afterwards Mrs. Burns gave birth to a son, named Francis Wallace, in compliment to Burns' steadfast friend, Mrs. Dunlop, who claimed descent from the Scottish Patriot. On the occasion of this birth, Burns' mother and sisters came to Ellisland, and affectionately nursed Mrs. Burns through her period of weakness and relieved her of the household and dairy duties. They brought with them the eldest son, Robert, now a boy of three years of age, who had, ever since his birth, resided with his grandmother and aunts, at Mossgiel. The warmest and most cordial love existed between Mrs. Burns, and the different members of her husband's family. In particular, she was affectionately attached to Burns' youngest sister, Isobel, afterwards Mrs. Begg, —then a bright intelligent girl, only four years her junior, and this attachment continued unbroken until it was severed by death, nearly half a century later.

The experiences of Burns and his wife at Ellisland were all that heart could desire. He was leading a quiet domesticated yet active life, and alike in body and mind was experiencing the full benefit of it, while his wife in the loving companionship of her husband, and in the sweet cares of her family and household, found all that her womanly nature required to fill to overflowing her cup of happiness. In a hitherto unpublished poem by Burns, communicated to us just as we were going to press, we have the following eloquent expression of contentment, love, and happiness, which formed the "home atmosphere" of the poet and his wife:

"To gild her worth I asked no wealthy dower,
  My toil could feed her, and my arm defend;
I envied no man's riches; no man's power,
  I asked of none to give, of none to lend.

And she the faithful partner of my care,
  When ruddy evening streaked the western sky;
Looked towards the uplands if her mate was there,
  Or through the beeches cast an anxious eye."

One loves to linger over the Ellisland period, for it formed undoubtedly the happiest episode of Burns' whole life, and who can fail to regret, not only for his sake, but also for his wife's, that it proved as brief as it was bright and happy. It endured for only three years, and during the whole of that period Burns is always seen at his best. His muse was never more prodigally responsive, and the finest effusions that he ever gave to the world were conceived in his placid domestic haven on the banks of the Nith. His *To Mary in Heaven; Tam o' Shanter;* and *Willie Brewed a Peck o' Maut;* form only a small part of his poetic productions at this time. His letters too have a dignity of expression, and an elevation and brilliancy of thought which indicate that all was well within, and the reason is very easy to divine. He was living in the midst of associations which satisfied, and satisfied fully, every aspiration of his soul; in his wife's affectionate society, and in the playful prattle of his children, he had, what was to him, a vital necessity; in his surroundings he had all that he could desire for the indulgence of his poetic communings with nature, while in the fellowship of intellectual and congenial friends, both in the neighborhood and from a distance, he had abundant opportunities of indulging

in his natural predilection for convivial social intercourse. Unfortunately, however, owing to his farm
proving unprofitable he is compelled to revert to his
excise commission which he had hitherto held in reserve. His application to be appointed to the
" Ride " in which he resided was successful but the
extra work this new duty entailed upon him was a
terrible drain on his natural vigour and energy. His
excise division embraced a wide tract of country
extending over ten parishes, and in one of his letters
written in November, 1790, he says: "I am jaded
to death with fatigue. For these two or three
months, I have not ridden less than 200 miles on an
average every week." Unfortunately, too, this
change in Burns' occupation entailed on him incessant and lengthened absences from home, and
from the society of his wife and children. Burns
must have felt this deprivation very keenly, for he
was a man of decidedly domestic habits and tastes,
and the chief happiness of his life always centred in
"those endearing connections consequent on the
venerable names of husband and father."

The glimpses afforded us of Mrs. Burns, at Ellisland, in her new position of wife and mother, are
disappointingly few and transient, but they all exhibit her as an active, industrious and frugal housewife; a kind, liberal and considerate mistress; a
devoted mother and an idolizing wife. There cannot be a doubt that she literally worshipped Burns,
and that in her devotion to him, she actually
attained to that lofty ideal, which forms the funda-
mental principal of truest loyalty—a belief that " he
could do no wrong." As an instance of this, reference may here be made to her truly noble act of
wifely self-abnegation in taking to her motherly
bosom and nursing, as a child of her own, the in-

fant "Betty," which "Anna wi' the gowden locks," had borne to Burns. The infant was born only ten days previous to the birth of her son, William Nicol Burns, in April, 1701, and as its unfortunate mother died in child-birth, Mrs. Burns adopted the motherless infant and nursed and fostered it, with all a mother's tenderness and care, until "Betty" reached the years of maturity, and became in her turn, a happy and devoted wife and mother. Yet so quietly and unassumingly was this act of unparalleled charity and generosity performed by Burns' noblehearted wife, that few—very few, were ever aware of the fact. Indeed, Mrs. Burns' own father, old Mr. Armour, if he ever knew of it at all, was ignorant of it at the time he visited his daughter at Ellisland, shortly after the birth of her child. On that occasion, he went forward and looked into the cradle, which his daughter was rocking, and on seeing *two* infants in it, he said in amazement—"I didna ken Jean, that you had twins again," and gently smiling, she simply replied,—"Neither I have faither, the ither bairn belongs to a friend, and I'm takin' care of it."

No doubt, amid all the community of feeling and loving sympathy and companionship which existed between her and her distinguished husband, there must have been frequent occasions, when his moods and thoughts soared far beyond her simple, practical ken, but on these occasions she always had the tact and delicacy to respect her husband's abstraction, and to wait the result in the truest spirit of conjugal love and confidence. We have good evidence of this, in her account of the composition of his immortal poem, *Tam o' Shanter*, in the end of the autumn of 1790. The poem was the work of one day, and she well remembered the circumstances.

Burns spent the most of the day on his favorite walk by the river, where in the afternoon she joined him with her two children. He was busily "croonin to himsel'," and perceiving that her presence was an interruption, she loitered behind with her little ones among the broom. Her attention was presently attracted by the wild gestures of the Bard, who, now at some distance was reciting aloud with tears of laughter rolling down his cheeks, some of the animated verses he had just conceived. Immediately afterwards the poem was committed to writing, on the top of a sod-dyke, at the water side, and when Burns came into the house, shortly afterwards, he read the verses in high "triumph to his wife, at the fireside." We have another similar instance occurring about the same period, the narrative being also taken from Mrs. Burns' own statement. "Burns though labouring under cold, spent the day in the usual work of the harvest, and apparently in excellent spirits, but as the twilight deepened he appeared to grow very sad, and at length wandered out into the barn-yard, to which his wife, in her anxiety, followed him, entreating him in vain to observe that frost had set in, and to return to the fireside. On being again and again urged, he promised compliance, but still remained where he was, striding up and down slowly, and contemplating the sky, which was singularly clear and starry. At last, Mrs. Burns found him stretched on a heap of straw, with his eyes fixed on a beautiful planet, that shone 'like another moon,' and pervailed on him to come in. He immediately, on entering the house, called for his desk, and wrote exactly as it now stands, with all the ease of one copying from memory, the sublime and pathetic *To Mary in Heaven*.

The displenishing sale at Ellisland proved a very

favourable one, and according to Mrs. Burns' statement they entered on their Dumfries experience with
a substantial sum in hand. Burns, besides, was
earning an annual salary of from £70 to £90, so
that they had what in those days, under Mrs. Burns'
careful and frugal management, might be regarded
as a fair provision for their station in life. The
dwelling they occupied, when they first came to
Dumfries, was the the second flat of a house in the
"Wee Vennel," now called Burns Street, in which
within the brief space of five years, the distinguished
Poet was doomed to breath his last. This house
consisted of two floors, and contained—a kitchen,
parlor, and two good bed-rooms, with several lesser
apartments. The change from rural life at Ellisland,
to town life in Dumfries, must have been as un-
pleasant for Mrs. Burns as it was great, but she was
endowed with that placidity of temper, and unvarying sweetness of disposition, which enabled her at
times to make the best of even the most unfavorable
circumstances—" Cribbed, cabined and confined "
in the little county town, she no doubt thought
often and longingly of their rural home at Ellisland,
and the comparative freedom and comfort of their
life there, with her household and dairy duties to interest her, and sweet periods of relaxation, as she
strolled with her husband and children among the
broom on the romantic banks of the Nith. These
retrospections, however, did not prevent her from
ministering with all her love and devotion to the
comfort and well-being of her husband and family.

To Burns, on the other hand, there is scarcely
room to doubt that the change of residence was a
pleasing and congenial one. He dearly loved the
companionship of his fellows, and the society in and
around Dumfries afforded him many opportunities

of gratifying those social tendences, which bulked so largely in his disposition. Much has been said as to his excesses during his residence in Dumfries, but it is now well understood that these have been greatly exaggerated, and we know that even at the worst they were never habitual in their character, nor did they interfere either with his capabilites as a business man, or with the proper discharge of his duty to his family. On the authority of an emphatic statement made by Mrs. Burns to her sister-in-law, Mrs. Begg, after the Poet's death, we learn that during the whole time of their residence in Dumfries " Burns never indulged, unless when he was in congenial company, and that although he was often out at convival meetings until a late hour, he never on a single occasion, however late he might be of coming home, failed in a custom he invariably observed before coming to bed, of going into the room where his children slept, and satisfying himself that they were all comfortably tucked in and sleeping soundly."

Burns' daily life in Dumfries must have been an active and busy one, for, besides his official duties, he was engaged, down almost to the very date of his death, in corresponding with Thomson in regard to the collection of Scottish songs, which Thomson was then editing, and in composing these matchless lyrics which have added so much lustre and fascination to our Scottish Minstrelsy. Burns' favourite walk at Dumfries was towards the Martingdon Ford, and here, according to Mrs. Burns, he composed many of his finest songs; and so soon as she heard him begin to "hum" to himself, she knew that he had something on his mind, and she was quite prepared to see him snatch up his hat, and set silently off for his favourite musing ground. The calls, too, on Burns' leisure hours were many and incessant, for besides associating continually with many families of position in and around Dumfries, his company was much in demand by many strangers of culture and eminence, who chanced to visit the district.

In the management of her domestic affairs, and in her intercourse with her husband's many friends and associates, Mrs. Burns continued to display, at Dumfries, the same prudence and unvarying, amiability which had characterized her at Ellisland, and six brief years passed over the heads of the household—six years of much comfort and happiness, although not unmingled too with trial and bereavement. About a year after their removal from Ellisland, Mrs. Burns gave birth to a daughter, named Elizabeth Riddell, after Burns' fair friend Mrs. Riddell, of Friars Carse, and about two years afterwards, she had a son, called James Glencairn in compliment to Burns' noble patron, the Earl of that name. About the time of this last mentioned birth, Burns and his wife had the grief to notice that their little girl was beginning to pine away, and after a protracted illness of more than a year, she died at Mauchline, where she had been sent in the hope of her health being improved by the change. Both of them were devotedly attached to their little daughter. Burns in particular was bound up in her, and one of the pleasing revelations we have of the Poet, is that handed down to us in the reminiscences of a native of Dumfries, who saw him often "sitting in the summer evenings at his door with this little child in his arms, dandling her, and singing to her, and trying to elicit her mental faculties."

The death occurred in the autumn of 1795, and the blow was intensified by the fact that Burns' own

health had become so undermined that he was
actually unable to go to Mauchline to see her interred. He was now frequently laid aside by protracted and severe illnesses, and in the following
year Mrs. Burns had the anguish to notice her distinguished husband's health becoming gradually
more and more shattered. Every remedy which her
love and devotion could suggest was tried, and at
times there appeared to be some slight symptom of
improvement, but it proved to be only temporary in
its character. For six sad weary months this continued, amid fluctuating hopefulness and disappointment, Mrs. Burns being much assisted in soothing
and nursing her dying husband, by their amiable
and warmly attached young friend Jessie Lewars:

> "Sweet as the smile when fond lovers meet,
> And soft as their parting tear."

As a last resource Burns was induced in the month
of July to go to Brow, a hamlet on the Solway Firth,
to try the effect of sea-bathing, but as Mrs. Burns
was again approaching confinement, she was unable
to accompany him. After ten days spent at Brow,
although decidedly benefited by the change, Burns
was seized by a restless longing to return home. As
stated in his own words—"he anxiously wished to
return to town, as he has not heard any news of
Mrs. Burns these two days." He accordingly returned to Dumfries, on Monday, 18th July, and by
his exposure during the long drive, an excess of
fever had set in, and on reaching his home he was
so weak as to be unable to stand upright. Weak
and ill as he was, he nevertheless contrived to pen
the following frantic appeal addressed to his father-
in-law, Mr. Armour, an appeal which, sad to say,
formed the last scrap of writing that was ever to
emanate from Burns' powerful and prolific pen:—

" DUMFRIES, MONDAY, 18th JULY, 1796.
MY DEAR SIR:

Do, for Heaven's sake, send Mrs. Armour here immediately. My wife is hourly expecting to be put to bed. Good God! what a situation for her to be in, poor girl, without a friend! I returned from sea-bathing quarters to-day, and my medical friends would almost persuade me that I am better but I think and feel that my strength is so gone that the disorder will prove fatal to me.

Your Son-in-law, R. B."

There is a deep, although melancholy satisfaction in thinking that this expiring effort of the mighty genius was actuated by his tender anxiety for his loving and devoted wife, and this feeling is intensified when we learn from Mrs. Burns' own statement that during his death agony, which set in very shortly after his arrival at his own house, he besought her to recall him to himself by touching him whenever she saw symtoms of his mind wandering What an amount of deep, solemn, heart filling gratification there is in the thought that the loving gentle touch of "his Jean " was the last sensation of which the dying Poet carried with him into the Realms of Eternity!

Burns' death occurred on the morning of Thursday, 21st July, 1796, and the interment took place on the Monday following, and on the same day his bereaved widow gave birth to a son, Maxwell Burns, who was ushered into this world while the bells of the churches were tolling his Father's funeral knell, and who survived his father barely three years.

Mrs. Burns survived her husband for fully thirty-eight years, and during the whole of that period she continued to occupy the house in which his life had so sadly and prematurely closed. Her existence although lonely, was far from being devoid of comfort and happiness. By the generous liberality of many of the admirers of her husband's genius, and by the proceeds realized from Dr. Currie's posthumous edition of the Poet's "Life and Works", her worldly comfort was amply provided for. Throughout her lengthened widowhood, she was regarded with general and genuine respect, not only on account of her association with the gifted Bard, but also on account of her own amiability of character: inherent good taste; and unvarying modesty of deportment.

For the memory of Burns she had an intense veneration, and she fondly cherished, to the very last, her every reminiscence of the brief but happy wedded life they had spent together. With all the loving tenderness of her single-hearted nature, she clung to the house in which he had lived and died, and although at the time she became a widow she was still an attractive, and comparatively speaking, a young woman, she refused to enter into a second marriage, although she had more than once an opportunity of doing so, decidedly to her wordly advantage. She devoted herself to the up-bringing and education of her children, refusing, firmly yet gratefully, in the hour of her greatest necessity, the offer of a generous kinsman of her husband, to relieve her of the maintenance and education of her eldest boy. As an instance too of her unselfish generosity, she refused to allow her brother-in-law, Gilbert Burns, to cast himself, and his mother and sisters on the world, by displenishing his farm, as he proposed to do, in order to pay up a debt of £180 which he owed to Robert, and which he knew was urgently required to provide for the wants of his brother's widow and children. Nor did her self-

sacrificing devotion to her fatherless family go unrewarded. It is true that her son, Maxwell, died
three years after her husband, at the age of three,
and four years thereafter, death also deprived her of
her son, Francis Wallace, in his fourteenth year, but
her eldest son Robert, gained for himself a good
position in the civil service, while her other two sons,
William and James, attained to distinguished military
rank, and ultimately retired as Lieutenant-Colonels
in the East India Company's Service. All of them
survived their mother for many years, but owing to
William and James being abroad, Robert, the eldest
son, was the only one who was privileged to witness
the closing scenes of their mother's life. We have
a touching and pathetic account of the death of
Mrs. Burns, furnished by her grand-daughter Sarah
Burns, now Mrs. Hutchinson, residing in Cheltenham,
the eldest daughter of Colonel James Glencairn
Burns. Mrs. Hutchinson, after the death of her
mother, in India, in 1821, was sent to this country
and consigned to the care of her grand-mother, by
whom she was tenderly and affectionately nurtured,
until death deprived her of her kind and venerable
guardian, in 1834. At that time Sarah was a mere
child of twelve, but she still retains, after a lapse of
more than half a century, a warm and fond recollection of her grand-mother. Being a day boarder at
a school at Dumfries, she saw little of her except
for an hour or two in the evening, owing to Mrs.
Burns being so disabled by paralysis, as to be unable to walk down stairs from her bed-room. Mrs.
Hutchinson says: "On Saturday afternoons when I
was home from school she used to give me pennies
to take round to some of her poor old neighbours,
and I remember the beggars who came to the door
always got meal to put into their 'pokes.' I can

only remember her kindness to me. I used to read a chapter to her out of the family Bible, and I can vividly remember seeing her, after her last seizure, lying speechless with her eyes closed. After our minister, Dr. Wallace prayed, she opened her eyes and looked round the room for me, and as I went beside her the tears coursed down her cheeks, and I think she pressed my hand, but she never spoke again." How thoroughly Jean's tender womanly heart went out towards the little motherless grand-daughter, who had been sent to brighten the closing years of her life, is evidenced by the fact that she expressly stipulated that her foster-daughter "Betty Burns" should name her youngest daughter "Sarah" after this idol of her old age. This touching fact is disclosed in a letter, which "Betty" wrote to her aunt Mrs. Begg, twelve years after her foster-mother's death, from which we cannot refrain from making the following quotation, as it affords the truest and most touching and genuine tribute that was ever paid to a good and generous hearted woman: "The names of the last two children, [Sarah Burns and James Burns], were all that Mrs. Burns exacted from me as an acknowledgement of her unwearied kindness to me. God was kind to her, my dear aunt, in giving her plenty but she did not hide it under a hedge: she willingly shared it with the poor and needy. The last letter I had from her was in July 1833, with £2 in it to buy a frock for my youngest child, then about a month old. The more I contemplate that excellent woman's character, the more I admire it. There was something good and charitable about her, sur-passing all women I ever yet met with. She was indeed a true friend, and the best of mothers to me, and I was often ready to think that all friendship for

me in the family had gone with her, but I am glad
to find it otherwise."

Mrs. Burns' death took place on Wednesday, 26th
March, 1834, shortly before midnight. She was
then in the 70th year of her age, and of this lengthened period, she had spent not less than forty-four
years in the town of Dumfries. As illustrating the
pleasing memories she left behind her there, we ex-
tract the following passages from a chaste tribute to
her, which appeared in the *Dumfries Courier*, of April 2, 1834, and which emanated from the pen of the
late Mr. M'Diarmind, an intimate personal friend of
Mrs. Burns, during the later period of her life:

"For more than 30 years, she was visited by thousands and thousands of persons, from the peer, down
to the itinerant sonneteer—the latter, a class of persons to whom she never refused an audience or dismissed unrewarded. Occasionally during the summer months, she was a good deal annoyed, but she
bore all in patience, and although naturally fond of
quiet, seemed to consider her house as open to visitors, and its mistress, in some degree, the property
of the public; but the attentions of strangers neither
turned her head, nor were ever alluded to in the
spirit of boasting.   *   *   *   *
" Hers, in short, was one of those well balanced
minds, that, cling instinctively to propriety, and a
medium in all things. Such as knew the deceased
earliest and latest, were unconscious of any change
in her demeanour and habits, except perhaps, greater
attention to dress and more refinement in manner,
insensibly acquired by frequent intercourse with
families of the first respectability. In her tastes,
she was frugal and simple, and delighted in music,
pictures and flowers. In spring and summer, it was
impossible to pass her windows, without being struck

by the beauty of the floral treasures they contained, and if extravagant in any way, it was in the article of roots and plants of the finest sorts. Fond of the society of young people, she mixed as long as able in their innocent pleasures, and cheerfully filled for them "the cup which cheers, but not inebriates." Although neither a sentimentalist, nor a blue stocking, she was a clever woman, possessed of great shrewdness, discriminating character admirably, and frequently made very pithy remarks,   *   *
*   *   *   When young, she must have been a handsome, comely woman, if not indeed a beauty, and up to middle life, her jet black eyes, were clear and sparkling. Her carriage was easy, and her step light. In ballad poetry her taste was good, and range of reading rather extensive. Her memory too was strong, and she could quote, when she chose, at considerable length and with great aptitude. Of these powers, the bard was so well aware that he read to her almost every piece he composed, and was not ashamed to own that he had profited by her judgement."

BONNIE JEAN.

HUNTER MacCULLOCH.
Author of "Robert Burns; A Centenary Ode."

(Air : Afton Water.)

When Scotia's ain song-bird, in life's leesome spring,
Flew 'round the braw birdies on bold, dashing wing,
An' whissled sae sweetly wi' sic winsome art,
They lookit an' listened an' tint was each heart.
There were Peggies an' Nannies an' Tibbies an' Nell,
Wha ower Rab the Ranter in turn cast a spell ;
Till the lowe o' true love, lit by sparklin' black een,
Bleezed up in his heart for his ae Bonnie Jean!

The stone-mason's lass was for lovin' designed,
Sae han'some her features, sae wholesome her mind;
In sweet-tempered Jean, wi' her kintra-bred life,
Scotia's ain darling bard fand his guid-willie wife.
An' weel for our Robin 'twas Jean that he wed,
Whase treasures were mair o' the heart than the head.
She lo'ed an' forgie'd him frae dawin till e'en;
Nae bird o' them a' could hae matched Bonnie Jean!

As his ain dearest jo, Bonnie Jean was his choice;
She charmed wi' her figure, her face an' her voice.
As a wife o' his ain, weel deserved she his rhyme,
Fu' worthy the happiest made "fireside clime."
She teaches her fatherless bairns, as she mourns,
To revere Scotia's chiefest o' bards, Robert Burns;
Whase memory she cherished till death closed her een;
Faithfu' maid, wife an' widow, all praise !
Bonnie Jean !

BONNIE JEAN IN EDINBURGH.

By Archibald Munro.

Reprinted from *The Scotsman*, January 23, 1894.

There have been many Bonnie Jeans, and it as safe to predict as it is pleasant to foresee that there will be many more; but there is only one on whom fortune has bestowed special distinction. All the others must be content to occupy a position subordinate to that of the one to whom the poetic genius of Robert Burns has procured a conspicuous niche in the Temple of Fame. A few general remarks on this celebrated heroine, and especially a brief account of her visit to Edinburgh, may not, perhaps, be out of place at a time when the minds of many people are being engaged with thoughts about an occasion when "a blast o' Januar' win' blew hansel in on Robin."

Though unhappily unacquainted with the advantages of the education which the enlightened conscience of the nation had provided for even the humblest ranks of the people, this excellent woman divined from attentive observation the benefits it confers on its fortunate possessors. No one was more anxious, therefore, to encourage a proposal to offer her eldest son a course of studies at a grammar school, and even at a university, notwithstanding her husband's satirical opinion of folk who enter college classes. Great was her satisfaction on hearing now and then from Robert Secundus accounts of his two years' experience at the Edinburgh University, as well as of his interviews with the notabilities who fraternised with his father in other days.

Brought up in the atmosphere of a district that

produced the worthies immortalized in the "Cottar's
Saturday Night," and nurtured under the roof of a
parent whose practice of the code of morality was
never disputed, Mrs. Burns was thoroughly con-
versant with the ideas and duties that appertain to
the highest interests of humanity.   To her family,
and to her husband also, she set an example of piety
by the observance of those sacred ordinances that
have given the Scottish peasantry an enviable no-
toriety among the nations of the earth.   During her
long widowhood of thirty-eight years she had the
sole charge of the up-bringing of her sons in the
way in which they should go, and right royally did
she face and discharge the responsibilities of her ex-
acting position.   The late Rev. Dr. Begg, who in
early youth was pastor of one of the Dumfries parish churches, had Mrs. Burns for one of his hearers,
and he used to dwell with great complacency on the
regularity of her attendance on his ministrations,
and on the fortunate coincidence that led to his acquaintance with the wife of one whom, in my own
hearing, he placed, in regard to greatness, above
all other Scotsmen, not excepting Bruce, Knox,
Scott, or even Chalmers.   Dr. Begg humorously related that while, in the course of his pastoral visits
to the widow's house, he was more eager to hear her
talk about her great husband than to discharge the
duty of the visiting pastor, she was prone to reverse
the order of things, and to confine the ecclesiastic to
his properly official track.   While he wanted reminiscences of Burns, his douce parishioner was fain to
crack about the Kirk.   On the termination of the
young preacher's connection with his Dumfries con-
gregation no member of his flock tendered a more
feeling regret than the shrewd and warm-hearted
relict of Robert Burns.

During her prolonged widowhood, Mrs. Burns continued to occupy the comparatively humble, but much frequented, house in which she had passed little more than a couple of the years of her married life. Pleased with her home, herself, and all the world besides she ne'er had changed nor wished to change her place, though often solicited by friends and relations at distance to enliven the monotony of her way of life by excursions hither and thither, or by a while's residence among them. Strange, to say, however, the lonely matron, when far advanced in years, yielded to the solicitations of friends to whom she was allied by no tie of blood. Some folk in Edinburgh, who had proved her most generous friends in the hour of her utmost need, expressed a wish that the consort of the boon companion who during his even brief sojourn among them had given their social life an interest unfelt before, and who, if it be true, as Walt Whitman opines, that the greatest city is that where the greatest man is found, made Edinburgh the capital of the country in a new sense, would enrich its associations by her presence among them. Entreaties from such a quarter and from such petitioners overbore Bonnie Jean's reluctance to leave the Queen of the South even for a day. Jean's visit to Edinburgh ought to be of considerable interest to all the readers of her husband's biography, all the more so, perhaps, that its particulars form no part of her recorded history. In the course of her journey towards the metropolis she had to pass a day or two at Mauchline, where she had an opportunity of seeing some of her own and her husband's now famous companions and acquaintances. James Humphreys, the noisy polemic of the village, rival of Burns himself in point of repartee, and the subject of possibly the severest epigram the poet ever put on paper; and John Lees, Burns' blackfoot at the Castle of Montgomery on the occasion of his visits to Highland Mary, and other cronies of scarcely less note in the poet's annals, waited on the illustrious visitor, and reviewed with her the characteristic scenes of many a social hour. All the Mauchline belles, of whom Jean herself was, as has been mentioned, the favourite of her husband's muse, were still in life, and, indeed, lived to a good old age—three of them being alive in the year 1851, a longevity which those who seek for causes to effects may be inclined to ascribe to the good humor infused into its possessors by the sprightly poetical compliments paid to them during their teens. Several of these "belles" were visited by the quondam Miss Armour as she proceeded to Edinburgh, and exchanged reminiscences with her of the happy era when they sat for the portraits which a master hand made of them respectively. To very few outsiders, however, were the interesting pilgrim's arrival and departure at and from the different localities through which she passed made known. This circumstance was in quite accordance with her own urgent request. This pre-arrangement was, as may be readily conjectured, a sore disappointment to many an admirer of her celebrated spouse.

Mrs. Burns' arrival in Edinburgh was soon made known to those family circles in which Burns may be said to have for several months lived, moved, and had his being. Mr. George Thomson, who had been the means of waking to new exertions the dormant muse of the national bard, and who had received, through correspondence, the first copies of those lyric gems on which the reputation of the author as a song writer chiefly rests, resided at the time of Mrs. Burns' visit in a tenement in the High

Street, adjoining the Exchange Square, and in the immediate vicinity of a room where Hugh Miller did editorial work for *The Witness.* The spot is therefore, as well as for more ancient considerations, time-honoured, and even classical. Mr. Thomson was among the most eager of the Edinburgh friends to see Bonnie Jean among them, and he coupled his request of a visit from her with a wish that she would make his house her home for the time being. With infinite delight the visitor was received by her host and family, the host pathetically declaring, after the preliminary greeting, that the greatest regret of his life was that circumstances stood in the way of his arranged meeting with her husband. Mr. Thomson frequently repeated the expression of this feeling in the course of his interviews with more recent relatives of the poet. One of the Mauchline belles, described by Burns as "Miss Smith, she has wit," in his lines on these heroines, was then resident in Nicolson Street, and was soon advised of the arrival of her fellow celebrity. At a later period this lady lived in South Charlotte Street, in the house of her distinguished son, the late Principal Candlish, and was, even in advanced life, as lively, cheerful, and witty as ever. In the year 1846 I had the pleasure of making the acquaintance of this great favorite of Burns, and drew from her society a new, and I hope instructive, interest in the peerless productions of her felicitous eulogist. Mrs. Candlish, who lost no time in calling on the companion of her girlhood, told her much of her own experience since 1785, when they were the toasts respectively of Robert Burns and James Candlish, and by her general knowledge and proverbial gifts, mightily interested Jean with her racy remarks on folk and fashions in Auld Reekie. Clarinda, too, the poet's

sometime goddess of the Potterrow, called and enchanted her adorer's widow with her well-known
fund of lore and charming powers of gossip to such
an extent that Bonnie Jean, by nature free from all
taint of envy or jealousy, became as much impressed
by her worth and sensibility as ever the impressionable poet himself had been, and facetiously pro-
nounced herself fortunate in possessing charms that
in the end triumphed over those of her talented and
pretty rival. How happy Robin was with either
when t' other was away! Other friends who had
visited Mrs. Burns in her home at Dumfries, and
still more who had not, came trooping to Mr.
Thomson's house to pay their respects, but did not
content themselves with leaving their cards. There
were daily levées of such friends as had known her
husband, or had interested themselves at his death,
in behalf of his widow and his little boys. Mr.
Robert Ainslie, W. S., the poet's companion during
his romantic excursions to the Border Counties, and
the witness of interesting revelations of his character, tender, douce, or gay; Dawnie Douglas, of
the Anchor Hotel, a howff which stood where the
Scotsman Office now stands, and where the
Crochallan Club was instituted, and, more noteworthy still, where Burns and his Edinburgh chums
had many a merry splore—these and other associates of the poet did themselves the honour of welcoming Bonnie Jean to "Scotia's darling seat." A
meeting between Mr. Walter Scott and Mrs Burns,
which, however, did not take place at Mr. Thomson's
house, was, probably, the one which all the students
of whatever is brillant and permanent in the poetry
and history of Scotland, must consider as the most
interesting episode in Mrs. Burns' visit to the Great
Wizard's "own romantic town." The matchless

novelist, who, when a boy, met Burns in Sheens House in circumstances which have engaged the pens of poets, and have lately occupied the thoughts and skill of one of our rising young painters, extended to Bonnie Jean a hand trembling all over with the emotions of tender memories. The interview was a protracted and affectionate one, the characteristics of the one friend most impressively affecting the mind and the heart of the other. Unfortunately for the interests of historical literature, Mrs. Burns' excessive modesty prevented her from letting the world know that part of the Wizard's remarks that related to the elder and more gifted son of the muse.

The catalogue of visitors would have been very incomplete indeed if it omitted the name of Mr. Alexander Cunningham, W. S., as generous a benefactor as ever relieved or cheered a bereaved family. This gentleman's worth and liberality has been reflected in fadeless characters in letters written to him by Burns. Almost the last letter the trembling hand of the dying poet penned was written to this, his best Edinburgh friend, and it ought to be a source of unmingled gratification to all sticklers for the fitness of things that the grandson of the Writer to the Signet, who bears his surname, has possession of the precious documents, and that very tempting offers have failed to induce him to part with them. They are, in truth, above price.

To what extent Mrs. Burns and her orphan family were indebted to Mr. Cunningham's zeal and munificence she and many others were well aware, and her grateful feelings found expression in the gift of probably the costliest relic of her immortal husband. A punchbowl of fine stone, made and presented by her father to the poet at the time of their happy reconciliation, was an article the daughter of the one and the wife of the other thought would be acceptable to the congenial associate of her husband. The punchbowl in after days fetched 300 guineas at a sale, and was, like Scotland's coronation stone, packed off to London to enrich the British Museum. Extravagant or at least sensational offers for the repurchase and recall of the precious memorial have not succeeded in restoring it to the Cunningham family. Had Mrs. Burns received no other kindness in Edinburgh beyond what she received at the residence of Mr. Cunningham, she was ready to declare that her husband had better friends than she gave him credit for, or than he even deserved.

Small parties were now and then formed in Mr. Thomson's house in honor of his guest. To these social gatherings scarcely any but the lovers of music and song were invited. Mr. Thomson, who was fellow-labourer with Burns in the composition of the work on Scottish melodies, was an accomplished violinist, and had taken his share in the entertainment of his company by discoursing excellent music on that instrument, with which he had been wont to charm the musical reunions of Cecilia's Hall at the foot of Niddry Street in the days of Schetki, Corelli, and Giornovichi, the Paganini of the period. The attention and hospitality of her host overcame any hesitation Mrs. Burns might have to exhibit her musical gifts in high Edinburgh society. Though the range of her gamut was not equal to what it had been, nor the tone so sympathetic as when her enraptured husband was the happiest of her audience, the romance of the occasion supplied what was awanting to the vocal spell. Some, indeed, declared that her acceptance as a singer needed no extrinsic consideration to commend it. Those songs that had been inspired by herself, and which after some gentle pressure she consented to sing, were listened to with an interest that could never again be revived in Edinburgh.

With all Mr. Thomson's admiration and study of the magnificent foreign musical compositions that were slowly working their way to British favour, he had a laudable predilection for Scottish lyrics, and no less a fancy for dance music. This was more in Jean's way. As a variation in the evening's enjoyments, a strathspey and reel occasionally followed the abstract attractions of choral harmonies. The younger members of the company generally monopolised the dancing accommodation of Mr. Thomson's limited apartments, and tripped it merrily to his cheery strains. Bonnie Jean, who seems to have been considered by all present too matronly to care for the fantastic mazes of her girlhood, was allowed to look on as a passive, perhaps a reluctant, spectator. At the close of a rattling reel one of the perspiring gymnasts advanced to Jean's chair, and jocularly remarked—"I suppose Mrs. Burns your dancing days are over?" "More than you seem to think so," roguishly responded the prima donna of old Mauchline penny reel days. "I have not seen you on the floor," gasped the embarrassed joker. "That's no fault of mine," replied the dame of nearly threescore summers. "Do you mean to say you would try a spring, Mrs. Burns?" "Ay, a dozen of them, gin I got the chance." Judge of the surprise and the delight of the company, including the fiddler and his wife, when they saw the venerable belle in her celebrated *role* stand up beside an ecstatic partner. Bonnie Jean's feet had lost none of their cunning. She set, she cleeked, and whirled about with a grace and agility that would have added new laurels to the fame of the beldame, whose gyrations in Auld Alloway Kirk enriched the een of Tam o' Shanter. Of course, every gallant present claimed Jean as his partner in the next dance. So thoroughly did the veteran danseuse enter into the spirit of the moment, and compel her fellow-dancers to bestir themselves, that not a few of them were right happy when the fiddler drew the last run of his bow. Bonnie Jean sat down smiling, and gaily hinted that she was ready to play a similar part in every subsequent night of her stay in her host's abode.

A visit to the theatre was proposed by Mr. Thomson, and cheerfully accepted by his light-hearted guest. At that time the theatre—the only one in the city—included in its orchestra a Mr. Fraser, who had acquired high reputation as a performer on the hautboy. As Fraser had played in the same house in the presence of Robert Burns himself some of the melodies that are married to his immortal verse, Mr. Thomson intimated to the popular musician that the widow of the poet was going to honour the playhouse with her patronage, and that it would be an appropriate compliment to her if on the occasion he would render one or more of those melodies that had delighted her husband in a former century. Fraser required no further suggestion; he was but too willing to honour himself by granting the favor asked. The air played was that of Burns' song, "Fee him, father, fee him," which as rendered by Fraser, in opposition to the popular interpretation of its sentiment, was not of a sprightly cast, but the echo of deep despair. The performer had been accustomed to treat the *habitués* of the theatre to this air, especially on his benefit nights; but as a special interest attached to the present occasion, he played with, if possible, more care and discrimination than ever. His pathetic notes drew tears from many eyes, even from those not usually given to the melting mood. To many individuals it appeared as if the performer brought Jean into the immediate presence of the spirit of her loving husband. It need hardly be added that she herself seemed to have been of the same opinion.

To Jean this pathetic song was charged with touching memories, of which neither Mr. Fraser nor any one of the crowded audience that listened to him had at that time any knowledge. Even Mr. Thomson was ignorant of their existence. The readers of the biographies of Burns may recollect that at a very dark period of the author's relation to Jean and her family he offered to become a toiler in her father's service, and remain in it till he discharged certain responsibilities supposed to be resting upon him. The song was, therefore, fitted, probably intended, to express the daughter's anxiety that her father should "fee" her lover in order, of course, that she might have more frequent opportunities of seeing him.

A round of other and various entertainments gladdened the heart of the stranger during her limited stay in the capital. On the eve of her withdrawal from Edinburgh, Mrs. Burns was honoured by her old and new friends with demonstrations of esteem and affection which even a Queen might consider herself fortunate in receiving from loyal and devoted subjects. On her return to Dumfries the much-longed-for lady was cordially welcomed back by all who knew her. Prominent among those who yearned for her return was Mrs. James Thomson, the Jessy Lewars of earlier days, and the subject of that imperishable beauty of verse and song, "O, wert thou in the cauld blast," the jointi nspiration of Burns and Mendelssohn.   To Mrs. Thomson there was sent by the hands of Mrs. Burns a message of esteem and gratitude from, among other friends, Sir Walter Scott, which might be regarded as a precious prelude to a more popular compliment paid to her on a later day.   Some of us who took a part in the famous Burns Festival held at Ayr in 1844 may remember the tumultous and prolonged applause that followed the mention by the Earl of Edinburgh in the banqueting pavilion near Alloway Kirk, of the services rendered by this the patient and devoted nurse of Burns during his last illness. On her return home, therefore, Mrs. Burns received from Mrs. Thomson more than a common welcome. Jean delighted to narrate, and Jessy delighted to hear of, the affectionate regard in which the deceased husband and friend was held in high quarters in the metropolis and elsewhere.

"OF A' THE AIRTS."

By The Rev. Arthur John Lockhart.

Author of " The Masque of Minstrels," etc.

There's a blur on the face of the late March moon;
The wind pipes shrill, and the chimneys croon;
Over our cottage it searching flies,
And every crack and cranny it tries;
From its wrestling might the elm springs free,
And it wings a wail from the willow tree.

But the wind of March, as I sit by the fire,
Plays through the heart's æolian lyre,
And to my listening spirit brings
The past and the future on its wings;—
The seer can see, and the singer sing,
When the wild March evening pipes of spring.

Then, as the firelight darts up clear,
And I see the guidwife sitting near,
A sweet auld song through my mind will go,—
"Of a' the airts the wind can blow;"
And the sweet home face, that is smiling seen,
Minds me right gaily of Bonnie Jean.

Rave, ye wild blast, and thou bright fire, glow!
" Of all the airts the wind can blow,
I dearly lo'e the wind o' the west
For there lives the lassie that I lo'e best:"
The heart that sings it throbs and yearns
With some of the passion of Robert Burns.

When the daisy blows, and the thrush appears,
One face comes peering across the years;
'Tis the face of him who toiled and sung,
When Jean was absent, and love was young,—
" I see her in the flowers sae fair,
I hear her voice as it charms the air."

Ah, fancy quikens! I see him stand
Alone in the field at Ellisland;
And all around him on every side,
The birds are singing at Whitsuntide;
But, though woods are green, and skies are gay,
There's a look in his eyes that is far away.

Then, in blissful dreaming, he moves along,
And he utters his heart in a joyous song:
" Wi' her in the west the wild woods grow;
The laverocks sing, and the rivers row;
And. though there's mony a hill between,
Ever my fancy is wi' my Jean.

" The winds may blow—the winds may blow—
Of a' the airts the wind can blow
The west is ever the dearest to me,
Till I my lassie again may see;
Greener the leaves, and the skies more sheen,
That hover over my Bonnie Jean."

She came, ere the winter, to ben an' byre;
She lit on the hearth her lover's fire;
Her smiles were like sunshine upon the walls;
Her words dropt sweet as the streamlet-falls;
The lassie of song was his wedded wife,
The heart he longed for was his for life.

O fortunate season, and hopeful time,
When the poet prospered in love and rhyme!
When, sowing or reaping, the day went by,
And he ploughed his fields, and tented his kye,
And he deemed, while the children played near his
     door,
That peace had come to depart no more.

O westlin' winds, full softly blow!
Ye bring content with your bloom or snow;
No more the poet's heart may roam
From fireside glow of his own calm home:
Would that, indeed, it had been so;—
Ye westlin' winds, full softly blow!

Ah, faithful Jean! there were other years!
For her were sorrows, for her were tears:
But the pansy weathers the wintry rime;
And she kept, as she might, her "fireside clime."
She lifted her burden,—her heart was stout,
And the lamp of her love, it never went out.

Ah, wayward brother, and poet wild!
With the shifting fancy of petted child,
And passionate spirit through dark eyes seen,—
Thou well might'st cherish and prize thy Jean!
Some fleeting favors the few might shed;
She loved thee living, and mourned thee dead.

What lyric queens in thy heart might reign,
Bemoaned with passion and tender pain:
She of the blind and the hopeless love;
And Mary, the sainted in Heaven above:—
Weeping, we sing of the rose-lip paled,
And the eyes soft glances so darkly veiled.

But one there was,—to her memory peace!
With thee she lieth in gray Dumfries;—
Hers were thy sorrows, successes, joys;
She cuddled thy lassies and reared thy boys;
She dropped o'er thy grave her quick hot tears,
And gave to thy memory her widowed years.

So when assemble the gay and young,
And songs of the Scottish land are sung,
And before the dreamer's raptured eye
The fair procession goes gliding by,
Not one of the haunted troop is seen
Dearer and truer than Bonnie Jean.

Stately in splendor, and radiant in light,
They thrill the ear, and they charm the sight;
They answer the music's melting call,—
But one is the jewel among them all:
Warmest, most human and gentle, appears
The patient woman who blessed his years.

And so, to-night, in my warm home-nest,
While the shrill March wind blows out of the west,
The auld sang hums through my musing brain,
Till I utter allowed the tender strain,—
And the guid wife sings by the firesides glow—
"Of a' the airts the wind can blow."

BURNS' BONNIE JEAN.

From Mrs. Jameson's "Loves of the Poets," (1844).

It was as Burns's wife as well as his early love, that Bonnie Jean lives immortalized in her poet's songs, and that her name is destined to float in music from pole to pole.   When they first met, Burns was about six-and-twenty, and Jean Armour "but a young thing,"

> Wi' iempting lips and roguish een,

the pride, the beauty, and the favourite toast of the village of Mauchline, where her father lived.   To an early period of their attachment, or to the fond recollection of it in after times, we owe some of Burns's most beautiful and impassioned song,—as

> Come, let me take thee to this breast,
>   And pledge we ne'er shall sunder !
> And I'll spurn as vilest dust
>   The world's wealth and grandeur, &c.

"O poortith cold and restless love;" "The kind love that's in her e'e;" "Lewis, what reck I by thee;" and many others.   I conjecture, from a passage in one of Burns's letters, that Bonnie Jean also furnished the heroine and the subject of that admirable song, "O whistle, and I'll come to thee, my lad," so full of buoyant spirits and artless affection: it appears that she wished to have her name introduced into it, and that he afterwards altered the fourth line of the first verse to please her:—thus,

> Thy Jeanie will venture wi' ye, my lad ;

but this amendment has been rejected by singers

and editors, as injuring the musical accentuation: the anecdote, however, and the introduction of the name, give an additional interest and a truth to the sentiment, for which I could be content to sacrifice the beauty of a single line, and methinks Jeanie had a right to dictate in this instance.* With regard to her personal attractions, Jean was at this time a blooming girl, animated with health, affection, and gaiety: the perfect symmetry of her slender figure; her light step in the dance; the "waist sae jimp," "the foot sae sma'," were no fancied beauties:— she had a delightful voice, and sung with much taste and enthusiasm the ballads of her native country; among which we may imagine that the songs of her lover were not forgotten. The consequences, however, of all this dancing, singing, and loving were not quite so poetical as they were embarrassing.

> O wha could prudence think upon,
> And sic a lassie by him?
> O wha could prudence think upon,
> And sae in love as I am?

Burns had long been distinguished in his rustic neighborhood for his talents, for his social qualities and his conquests among the maidens of his own rank. His personal appearance is thus described from memory by Sir Walter Scott:—"His form was strong and robust, his manner rustic, not clownish; with a sort of dignified simplicity, which received part of its effect, perhaps, from one's knowledge of his extraordinary talents; * * * his eye alone, I think, indicated the poetical character and temperament; it was large, and of a dark cast, which

---

* "A Dame whom the graces have attired in witchcraft, and whom the loves have armed with lightning—a fair one—herself the heroine of the song insists on the amendment—and dispute her commands if you dare."—Burns' Letters.

glowed, (I say literally, glowed) when he spoke with feeling and interest. His address to females was extremely deferential, and always with a turn either to the pathetic or humorous, which engaged their attention particularly. I have heard the late Duchess of Gordon remark this;" and Allan Cunningham, speaking also from recollection, says, "he had a very manly countenance, and a very dark complexion; his habitual expression was intensely melancholy, but at the presence of those he loved or esteemed, his whole face beamed with affection and genius;" *** "his voice was very musical; and he excelled in dancing, and all athletic sports which required strength and agility."

It is surprising that powers of fascination which carried a Duchess "off her feet," should conquer the heart of a country lass of low degree? Bonnie Jean was too softhearted, or her lover too irresistible; and though Burns stepped forward to repair their transgression by a written acknowledgement of marriage, which, in Scotland, is sufficient to constitute a legal union, still his circumstances, and his character as a " wild lad," were such, that nothing could appease her father's indignation; and poor Jean, when humbled and weakened by the consequences of her fault and her sense of shame, was prevailed on to destroy the document of her lover's fidelity to his vows, and to reject him.

Burns was nearly heart-broken by this dereliction, and between grief and rage was driven to the verge of insanity His first thought was to fly the country; the only alternative which presented itself, " was Jamaica or a jail;" and such were the circumstances under which he wrote his " Lament," which, though not composed in his native dialect, is poured forth

with all that energy and pathos which only truth
could impart.

> No idly feigned poetic pains,
>   My sad, love lorn lamenting claim ;
> No shepherd's pipe—Arcadian strains,
>   No fabled tortures, quaint and tame :
> The plighted faith—the mutual flame—
>   The oft-attested powers above—
> The promised father's tender name—
>   These were the pledges of my love !

This was about 1786 : two years afterwards, when
the publication of his poems had given him name
and fame, Burns revisited the scenes which his
Jeanie had endeared to him : thus he sings exult-
ingly,—

> I'll aye ca' in by yon town
> And by yon garden-green, again :
>   I'll aye ca' in by yon town,
> And see my Bonnie Jean again !

They met in secret; a reconciliation took place;
and the consequences were that Bonnie Jean, being
again exposed to the indignation of her family, was
literally turned out of her father's home.   When
the news reached Burns he was lying ill; he was
lame from the consequences of an accident,—the
moment he could stir, he flew to her, went through
the ceremony of marriage with her in presence
of competent witnesses, and few months afterwards
he brought her to his new farm at Ellisland, established her under his roof as his wife, and the
honoured mother of his children.
    It was during this second-hand honeymoon,
happier and more endeared than many have proved
in their first gloss, that Burns wrote several of the
sweetest effusions ever inspired by his Jean; even in

the days of their early wooing, and when their intercourse had all the difficulty, all the romance, all the mystery, a poetical lover could desire. Thus practically controverting his own opinion, " that conjugal love does not make such a figure in poesy as that other love," &c.—for instance, we have that most beautiful song, composed when he left his Jean at Ayr (in the west of Scotland,) and had gone to prepare for her at Ellisland, near Dumfries.

> " Of a' the airts the wind can blaw,
>   I dearly like the west,
> For there the bonnie lassie lives,
>   The lassie I lo'e best :
> There wild woods grow, and rivers row,
>   And monie a hill between ;
> But day and night my fancy's flight
>   Is ever wi' my Jean.
>
> I see her in the dewy flowers,
>   I see her sweet and fair :
> I hear her in the tunefu' birds,
>   I hear her charm the air :
> There's not a bonnie flower that springs
>   By fountain, shaw, or green ;
> There's not a bonnie bird that sings,
>   But minds me o' my Jean."

Nothing can be more lovely than the luxuriant, though rural imagery, the tone of placid but deep tenderness, which pervades this sweet song; and to feel all its harmony, it is not necessary to sing it—it is music in itself. In November, 1778, Mrs. Burns took up her residence at Ellisland, and entered on her duties as a wife and mistress of a family, and her husband welcomed her to her home ("her ain roof-tree,") with the lively, energetic, but rather unquotable song, "I hae a wife o' my ain;" and subsequently he wrote for her, " O were I on Parnassus Hills," and that delightful little bit of simple feeling—

She is a winsome wee thing,
She is a handsome wee thing,
She is a bonnie wee thing,
　　This sweet wee wife of mine.
I never saw a fairer,
I never lo'ed a dearer,—
And next my heart I'll wear her,
　　For fear my jewel tine !

and one of the finest of all his ballads, "Their
groves o' Sweet myrtle," which not only presents a
most exquisite rural picture to the fancy, but
breathes the very soul of chastened and conjugal
tenderness.

I remember, as a particular instance—I suppose
there are thousands—of the tenacity with which
Burns seizes on the memory, and twines round the
very fibres of one's heart, that when I was traveling
in Italy, along that beautiful declivity above the
river Clitumnus, languidly enjoying the balmy air,
and gazing with no careless eye on those scenes of
rich and classical beauty over which memory and
fancy had shed

A light, a glory, a fair luminous cloud
Enveloping the earth ;

even then, by some strange association, a feeling of
my childish years came over me, and all the livelong
day I was singing, sotto voice—

There's groves o' sweet myrtle let foreign lands reckon,
　　Where bright-beaming summers exalt the perfume ;
Far dearer to me yon lone glen o' gran bracken,
　　Wi' the burn stealing under the long yellow broom !
Far dearer to me are yon humble broom bowers,
　　Where the blue-bell and gowan lurk lowly unseen,
For there, lightly tripping among the wild flowers,
　　A' listening the linnet, oft wanders my Jean.

Thus the heath, and the blue-bell, and the gowan,

had superseded the orange and the myrtle on those Elysian plains,

Where the crush'd weed sends forth a rich perfume.

And Burns and Bonnie Jean were in my heart and on my lips, on the spot where Virgil had sung, and Fabius and Hannibal met.

Besides celebrating her in verse, Burns has left us a description of his Bonnie Jean in prose. He writes (some months after his marriage) to his friend Miss Chalmers,—"If I have not got polite tattle, modish manners, and fashionable dress, I am not sickened and disgusted with the multiform course of boarding-school affectation; and I have got the handsome figure, the sweetest temper, the soundest constitution, and the kindest heart in the country. Mrs. Burns believes, as firmly as her creed, that I am le plus bel esprit, et le plus honnete homme in the universe; although she scarcely ever in her life, (except reading the Scriptures and the Psalms of David in metre) spent five minutes together on either prose or verse, I must except also a certain late publication of Scots Poems, which she has perused very devoutly, and all the ballads in the country, as she has (O' the partial lover! you will say) the finest woodnote wild I ever heard."

After this, what becomes of the insinuation that Burns made an unhappy marriage,—that he was " compelled to invest her with the control of his life, whom he seems at first to have selected only for the gratification of a temporary inclination;" and "that to this circumstance most of his misconduct is to be attributed?" Yet this, I believe, is a prevalent impression. Those whose hearts have glowed, and whose eyes have filled with delicious tears over the songs of Burns, have reason to be grateful to Mr.

Lockhart, and to a kindred spirit, Allan Cunningham, for the generous feeling with which they have vindicated Burns and his Jean. Such aspersions are not only injurious to the dead and cruel to the living, but they do incalculable mischief:—they are food for the flippant scoffer at all that makes the "poetry of life." They unsettle in gentler bosoms all faith in love, in truth, in goodness—(alas, such disbelief comes soon enough!) they chill and revolt the heart, and "take the rose from the fair forehead of an innocent love to set a blister there."

"That Burns," says Lockhart, "ever sank into a toper, that his social propensities ever interfered with the discharge of the duties of his office, or that, in spite of some transitory follies, he ever ceased to be a most affectionate husband,—all these charges have been insinuated, and they are all false. His aberrations of all kinds were occasional, not systematic; they were the aberrations of a man whose moral sense was never deadened—of one who encountered more temptations from without and from within, than the immense majority of mankind, far from having to contend against, are even able to imagine," and who died in his thirty-sixth year, "ere he had reached that term of life up to which passions of many have proved too strong for the control of reason, though their mortal career being regarded as a whole, they are honoured as among the most virtuous of mankind."

We are told also of "the conjugal and maternal tenderness, the prudence and the unwearied forbearance of his Jean," and that she had much need of forbearance is not denied; but he ever found in her affectionate arms, pardon and peace, and a sweetness that only made the source of his occasional delinquencies sting the deeper.

She still survives (1844) to hear her name, her early love, and her youthful charms, warbled in the songs of her native land. He, on whom she bestowed her beauty and her maiden truth, dying, has left to her the mantle of his fame. What though she be now a grandmother? to the fancy, she can never grow old, or die. We can never bring her before our thoughts but as the lovely, graceful country girl, "lightly tripping among the wild flowers," and warbling, "Of a' the airts the win' can blaw,"—and this, O women, is what genius can do for you! Wherever the adventurous spirit of her countrymen transport them, from the spicy groves of India to the wild banks of the Mississippi, the name of Bonnie Jean is heard, bringing back to the wanderer sweet visions of home, and of days of "auld lang syne." The peasant-girl sings it "at the ewe milking," and the high-born fair breathes it to her harp and her piano. As long as love and song shall survive, even those who have learned to appreciate the splendid dramatic music of Germany and Italy, who can thrill with rapture when Pasta,

> Queen and enchantress of the world of sound,
> Pours forth her soul in song ;

or when Sontag,

> Carves out her dainty voice as readily
> Into a thousand sweet distinguished tones,

even them shall still have a soul for the "Banks and Braes o' Bonnie Doon," still keep a corner of their hearts for truth and nature—and Burns's Bonnie Jean.

FAITHFUL JEAN.

By the Rev. Arthur John Lockhart.

As one, who doth the skyey realm survey,—
Who hails, in radiant constancy, afar
O'er night's blue-tower, the sailor-guiding star,—
Is gladdened by Sélén's silver ray,
Ris'n o'er her hill upon some rippling bay;
So he, whose poet-eyes were wandering still
Where maiden charms his fiery soul would fill
With passion to inspire his living lay,—
To carol love of Mary,—musing song
Of perfect sorrow o'er her early tomb,—
To chant the Ballochmyle at dewy e'en,—
Maria's call the twilight woods among,—
Jessy and Nannie, in their sweetest bloom,—
Found cheer in the bright face of Bonnie Jean.

THE WIFE OF BURNS.

By Alan Scott.

When in wintry January the birthday of Robert Burns comes round, and the hearts of all true Scotsmen turn in pride to their greatest poet, my heart always chivalrously inclines to his wife. What a clever woman she must have been to have filled so well the position of wife to the greatest genius of her time! The wife of another great genius of later days has given us clearly to understand the difficulty of such a lot. Unlike her, Bonnie Jean never realised the greatness of her task and therefore did not seek to magnify her office. That she managed beautifully for all that is undoubted.

What a dainty picture she makes, the soft, sonsy little woman, wholesome and sweet as her own pats of golden butter! Not a single harsh line is there in her aspect; all is toned with kindly feeling. The round, comely face is kept youthful by good humor, the eye is ever ready to dart its pawky glance at the saucy joke of a friend, and the plump little hand to welcome the stranger with a cantiness becoming the mistress of Ellisland. What music there is in her voice too—suggestions of all the sweet song of a long summer day, from the blythe lilt of the haymakers to the soft crooning of the milkmaids when the kye come hame in the gloaming! Her laugh— the echo of the gigantic laughter of the shrewd, keen-witted farmers of old Coila—is fresh and vigorous as the breezes that blow o'er the moorlands of Ayrshire. But her dearest charm is her domestic manner. As you watch her trotting but and ben between pantry and dairy and kitchen, keeping the cradle rocking with a touch of her foot as she passes to and fro, you are reminded of departed generations of notable housewives—women who rose morning after morning "wi' the skreigh o' day," whose ambition it was to have the best butter in the market, who spent their days in milking and churning to that end, and their evenings in spinning, or, as George Eliot quaintly says, "laying up linen for the life to come." Old-fashioned, cheery, plump little woman! I can imagine no more suitable wife for a poet, she being no poetess—rather a poem in herself.

But did she quite understand her man of genius? Perhaps not. Perhaps she never read the full meaning of his glorious eyes. Perhaps to the very last he was only the wittiest man in the parish, quicker with tongue and pen than either minister or schoolmaster, and with a wonderful knack of making rhymes. Certainly she never thought him too glorious to be scolded when he came home late on market days, or coaxed out of a moody fit with a blythe song. Still, he always held the first place in her heart as the lover of her youth, and was more to her than she was to him.

And did Robert Burns miss anything in his Bonnie Jean? Did he ever wish for a fuller sympathy in the wife of his choice? Very likely he did. Most men hanker after what they cannot get. Even the chivalrous Ivanhoe sighed for the dark eyes of Rebecca while he gazed into the blue ones of Rowena. But, unlike many men, our poet was too kind-hearted and delicate to let his wife feel aught of this. Besides, if he ever gave himself up to a contemplation of the woman he *might* have married he would have risen consoled not regretful. He might, for instance, have married a sweet, angelic woman who, instead of scolding him, would have pined away into grief when brought in contact with the failings of his human nature. He might have been united to one of your angular women, and had his peace wrecked against the principles, proprieties, and peculiarities of her three-cornered character. He might have wedded a tragedy-queen like Clarinda, from whose high sentiment he might have lived, like a man in a balloon, in constant danger of an explosion. And, worst of all, he might have had an intellectual wife, who would have worn herself out in worshipping and mocking him alternately, as the different phases of his many-sided character presented themselves to her view, and who, to a dead certainty, would have written a diary! As for us who, among his admirers, think regretfully of Highland Mary, let us remember that from all accounts she was of the angelic type, and therefore more fitted to be his guardian angel in Heaven, while Jean was undoubtedly more capable of looking after his temporal interests on earth. Yes! there is much to sadden us in the life of Robert Burns, but this one comfort remains; he married a healthy cheery, active woman—a daughter, as he was a son, of the people. She did not spoil his life, and I daresay he did not spoil hers, though I cannot think he would be altogether an exemplary husband, seeing he had not the privilege of reading the enlightened literature, which is addressed to the young married men now-a-days. I can even imagine his Bonnie Jean being a little disappointed in him—for all of us life is something less than we expect—but I cannot think he would ever be hard with her. He was too conscious of his failings to take note of other people's. (From perfect men, good Lord, deliver us!) And he did wake up to her charms sometimes, else we should have missed some of our loveliest lyrics.

Women are said to be like flowers. They are rare
flowers that bloom in wondrous beauty, and are a
continual source of pleasure and gratification to
their admirers. And there are in old-fashioned
gardens uninteresting herbs that you would pass by
if it were not for the faint fragrance they exhale.
Ah! these are the flowers that have memories.
There is rosemary, that's for remembrance. You
pluck it and lay it aside for ever so long, away from
the light. But when you take it out and press it the
sweet fragrance greets you once more, and you are
reminded of the old-fashioned garden and the sunshine and light. Women are like flowers, they have
different charms. There are two women I cannot
help associating in my mind—the wife of Carlyle
and the wife of Burns. Carlyle's wife was a woman
of rare attainments, admired by many of the gifted
men of her time, the great glory and pride of the
most gifted of all. This lesser Jeanie of ours was
scarcely heard of while she made home for the
great Poet of the People; but now, after long years,
you have only to mention her name and you will recall the music of many of Scotland's sweetest songs.

BONNIE JEAN IN HER OLD AGE.

Mr. James Mackenzie tells in a recent number of the *Scots' Magazine*, that his father, who was one of the founders of the Royal Scottish Academy, painted Burns' "Bonnie Jean" when nearing her 7oth year. "He found her to be a woman of much originality, and of rare open-heartedness and benevolence. And yet he thought it likely enough that Burns may have been captivated more by her personal than her mental attractions; because it was evident that she must have been, if not beautiful, certain very comely of feature, and her form must have been superb. Her figure was admirable, even in old age.

HOW HEW AINSLIE KISSED JEAN ARMOUR.

By Thomas C. Latto.

Before Ainslie left for America, he had a great desire to pay what he called his "devours" to Mistress Jean Armour. On arriving at Dumfries, he visited Burns's grave, and then sought Mrs. Burns's humble cottage. After a pleasant "twa-handed crack," they walked together to Lincluden Abbey, and Mrs. Burns paused on a sheltered and lovely spot. "It was just here," she said, "that my man often paused, and I believe made up many a poem an' sang ere he cam' in to write it down. He was never fractious—aye good-natured and kind baith to the bairns and to me." On parting, Ainslie said to her, "I wad like weel ere I gae, if ye wad permit me, to kiss the cheek o' Burns's faithful Jean, to be a reminder to me o' this meeting when I am far awa'." She laughed, and holding up her face to him, said, "Aye, lad, an' welcome." So she and Burns's fervent disciple parted, he to America, in his own words, "to seek for themselves and friends a resting-place in the young world of the West, where those seeds of freedom and independence that 'the voice of Coila' had sown in their souls might flourish and bloom, unstinted by the poisonous pruning of despots or the deadly mildew of corruption."

> " Noo, Jeanie, that we've daunert by
> Scenes dear to *him* an' you, lass,
> A sudden thocht starts in my head—
> Na! frae the heart, I trow, lass.

O, micht I daur, ere pairt for aye,
  Frae ane I'm thirl'd to lo'e, lass,
Bear ower the sea a memory,
  Kiss o' thy bonnie mou', lass?

"Where one great Muse, 'mang cushie-doos
  Once roam'd, love ditties broodin',
We've wander'd in the wavin' wuds
  That scourge thy wa's, Lincluden;
Yet let a laddie, wha has left
  His Bourocks o' Bargeny,
Tak' sic a precious boon, for ance,
  And only ance, dear Jeanie."

The dear old dame, nae thocht o' shame,
  In her saft e'e a twinkle,
Held up her snappy lips, untouched
  By ae unseemly wrinkle;
"Oo aye," she said, "an' welcome, lad,
  It's a' that I can gie thee,
But gin it do thee ony guide,
  My man, then tak' it wi' thee."

MRS. BURNS.

From Cunningham's "Life and Land of Burns," (1841.)

> "There's not a bonnie flower that springs,
>   By fountain, shaw, or green,—
> There's not a bonnie bird that sings,
>   But minds me o' my Jean.

When Bishop Percy lamented that there were few songs in our language expressing the joys of wedded love, Burns was a lad some two and twenty years old; but though his life was brief, he lived long enough to hinder Percy's remark from continuing proverbial, and gladdened our firesides with strains dedicated to household love, which live in every heart, and are heard from every tongue.

Few of our poets have been happy in their wives; Shakespeare neglected his, and all but forgot her in his will; Milton, though more than once married, was unable to find that domestic quiet which, perhaps his own nature prevented him from obtaining; the poems of Dryden bear witness to the unhappiness of his choice, for the sharpness of his satire has an additional edge when a fling can be had at matrimony; and Addison sought the comfort abroad, which his wife, the Dowager Countess of Warwick, denied him at home. To this the wife of Burns, the "bonnie Jean" of many a far-famed song, was an exception; she was a country girl of the west of Scotland, remarkable for the elegance of her person and the sweetness of her voice. Her father was a respectable Master-Mason in Mauchline, in good employment, and with a family of eleven children. Jean was born in February 1765, and was, when

Burns became intimate with her but newly out of her teens. How her aquaintance with the poet began, she loved to relate:—she had laid some linen webs on the grass to bleach, and while sprinkling them with water from a neighboring burn, a favorite collie of the poet's ran across them, staining them with its feet, to fawn upon her; she struck at the dog, when Burns stepped forward, and reproached her in the words of Allan Ramsay:—

" E'en as he fawned, she strak the poor dumb tyke."

The fair bleacher smiled, and an aquaintance commenced, which a country place like Mauchline afforded many opportunities to promote.

This ripened into love; she was united to Burns, and during his too short life, bore to him four sons and five daughters, three of whom, and these all men, survive. She was a kind and dutiful wife, an affectionate mother, and a good neighbor. All who knew her liked her; and though country bred, and with moderate education, she was not wanting in conversation fit for the most accomplished, and left an impression of her good sense on the many strangers, who, like pilgrims to a shrine, went to see her for the sake of the Bard. It should be added, that she danced with grace and neatness, and sang, moreover, Scottish songs with a spirit, a feeling, and a sweetness but seldom found together. " She has," says Burns to Miss Chalmers, "the finest wood-note-wild I ever heard." The two best songs which her charms called forth are those beginning—

" Of a' the airts the win' can blaw,"
and
" O were I on Parnassus' hill."

The former was written, as he himself tells us, during the honey moon; and what a glorious welcome to the new farm does the latter contain! Had he welcomed her to Hagley or to Stowe, the strain could not have come more freely from the heart, or had more of passion or of poetry about it. One of these alone had been enough to have embalmed the name of Mistress in song; but the two together have immortalized a wife.

But there are other songs, excellent of their kind, and only inferior in beauty because they cannot abide comparisim with things perfect, that record the beauty of Jean Armour. How exquisite is this brief strain—the finest essences are held in the smallest bottles:—

> "Louis, what reck I by thee,
>   Or Geordie on his ocean?
> Dyvor, beggar-loons to me—
>   I reign in Jeanie's bosom.
>
> Let her crown my love her law,
>   And in her breast enthrone me;.
> Kings and Nations—swith, awa'!
>   Reif randies, I disown ye!"

Jean Armour, whose name has no chance of passing from earth, died on Wednesday, the 26th of March, 1834, and was buried by the side of her husband, whom she had survived nearly eight-and-thirty years.

THE WIFE OF BURNS.

By John Gibson Lockhart.

" To make a happy fireside clime
For weans and wife,
That's the true pathos and sublime
Of human life."

Burns, as soon as his bruised limb was able for a journey, rode to Mossgiel, and went through the ceremony of a Justice-of Peace marriage with Jean Armour, in the writing-chambers of his friend Gavin Hamilton. He then crossed the country to Dalswinton, and concluded his bargain with Mr. Miller as to the farm of Ellisland, on terms which must undoubtedly have been considered by both parties as highly favorable to the poet; they were indeed fixed by two of Burn's old friends who accompanied him for that purpose from Ayrshire. The lease was for four successive terms, of nineteen years each,—in all seventy-six years; the rent for the first three years and crops £50; during the remainder of the period £70. Mr. Miller bound himself to defray the expenses of any plantations which Burns might please to make on the banks of the river; and the farmhouse and offices being in a dilapidated condition, the new tenant was to receive £300 from the proprietor for the erection of suitable buildings. " The land," says Allan Cunningham, " was good, the rent moderate, and the markets rising."

Burns entered on possession of his farm at Whitsuntide 1788, but the necessary rebuilding of the house prevented his removing Mrs. Burns thither until the season was far advanced. He had, moreover, to qualify himself for holding his Excise commission by six weeks' attendance on the business of that profession in Tarbolton. From these circumstances, he had this summer a wandering and unsettled life, and Dr. Currie mentions this as one of his chief misfortunes. "The poet," as he says, "was continually riding between Ayrshire and Dumfriesshire; and, often spending a night on the road, sometimes fell into company and forgot the good resolutions he had formed."

What these resolutions were the poet himself shall tell us. On the third day of his residence at Ellisland, he thus writes to Mr. Ainslie: "I have all along hitherto, in the warfare of life, been bred to arms, among the light horse, the piquet guards of fancy, a kind of hussars and Highlanders of the brain; but I am firmly resolved to sell out of these giddy battalions. Cost what it will, I am determined to buy in among the grave squadrons of heavy-armed thought, or the artillery-corps of plodding contrivance. * * Were it not for the terrors of my ticklish situation respecting a family of children, I am decidedly of opinion that the step I have taken is vastly for my happiness."

To all his friends he expresses himself in terms of similar satisfaction in regard to his marriage. "Your surmise, madam," he writes to Mrs. Dunlop (July 10th), "is just. I am indeed a husband. I found a once much-loved, and still much-loved female, literally and truly cast out to the mercy of the naked elements, but as I enabled her to purchase a shelter, and there is no sporting with a fellow-creatures happiness or misery. The most placid good-nature and sweetness of disposition; a warm heart, gratefully devoted with all its powers to love

me; vigorous health and sprightly cheerfulness, set
off to the best advantage by a more than commonly
handsome figure; these, I think, in a woman, may
make a good wife, though she should never have
read a page but the Scriptures of the Old and New
Testament, nor danced in higher assembly than a
penny-pay wedding   *   *   To jealousy or infidelity I am, an equal stranger; my preservative
from the first, is the most thorough consciousness of
her sentiments of honor, and her attachment to me;
my antidote against the last, is my long and deep-
rooted affection for her.   In housewife matters, of
aptness to learn, and activity to execute, she is eminently mistress, and during my absence in Nithsdale, she is regularly and constantly an apprentice
to my mother and sisters in their dairy, and other
rural·business.   *   *   You are right that a
bachelor state would have ensured me more friends;
but from a cause you will easily guess, conscious
peace in the enjoyment of my own mind, and un-
mistrusting confidence in approaching my God,
would seldom have been of the number."

Some months later, he tells Miss Chalmers that his
marriage "was not, perhaps, in consequence of the
attachment of romance," he is addressing a young
lady—"but," he continues, "I have no cause to repent it.   If I have not got polite tattle, modish manners, and fashionable dress, I am not sickened and
disgusted with the multiform curse of boarding-
school affectation; and I have got the handsomest
figure, sweetest temper, the soundest constitution,
and the kindest heart in the country.   Mrs. Burns
believes as firmly as her creed, that I am "le plus
esprit et le plus honnet homme" in the universe;
although she scarcely ever, in her life, except the
Scriptures and the Psalms of David in metre, spent

five minutes together on either prose or verse—I must except also a certain late publication of Scotch Poems, which she has perused very devoutly, and, all the Ballads of the country, as she has (O the partial lover you will say) the finest wood-note-wild I ever heard."

It was during this honeymoon, as he calls it, while chiefly resident in a miserable hovel at Ellisland, and only occasionally spending a day or two in Ayrshire, that he wrote the beautiful song—

> "Of a' the airts the wind can blaw,
>   I dearly like the west ;
> For there the bonnie lassie lives,
>   The lassie I lo'e best ;
> There wild-woods grow, and rivers row,
>   And mony a hill between ;
> But day and night my fancy's flight
>   Is ever wi' my Jean.
>
> I see her in the dewy flowers,
>   I see her sweet and fair :
> I see her in the tunefu' birds,
>   I hear her charm the air ;
> There's not a bonnie flower, that springs,
>   By fountain, shaw, or green ;
> There's not a bonnie bird that sings,
>   But minds me o' my Jean."

"A discerning reader," says Mr. Walker, "will perceive that the letters in which he announces his marriage to some of his most respected correspondents, are written in that state when the mind is pained by reflecting on an unwelcome step, and finds relief to itself in seeking arguments to justify the deed, and lessen its advantages in the opinion of others." I confess I am not able to discern any traces of this kind of feeling in any of Burns's letters on this interesting and important occasion. Mr. Walker seems to take it for granted, that because Burns admired the superior manners and accomplishments of women of the higher ranks of society, he must necessarily, whenever he discovered "the interest which he had the power of creating" in such persons, have aspired to find a wife among them. But it is, to say the least of the matter, extremely doubtful, that Burns, if he had had a mind, could have found any high-born maiden willing to partake sucn fortunes as his were likely to be, and yet possessed of such qualifications for making him a happy man, as he had ready for his acceptance in his "Bonnie Jean." The proud heart of the poet could never have stooped itself to woo for gold; and birth and high-breeding could only have been introduced into a farmhouse to embitter, in the upshot, the whole existence of its inmates. It is very easy to say, that had Burns married an accomplished woman, he might have found domestic evenings sufficient to satisfy all the cravings of his mind—abandoned tavern haunts and jollities for ever—and settled down into a regular pattern-character. But it is at least as possible, that consequences of an exactly opposite nature might have ensued. Any marriage, such as Professor Walker alludes to, would, in his case, have been more unequal than either of those that made Dryden and Addison miserable for life. Sir Walter Scott, in his "Life of Dryden" (p. 90), has well described the difficult situation of her who has "to endure the apparently causeless fluctuation of spirits incident to one doomed to labour incessantly in the feverish exercise of the imagination. Unintentional neglect," says he, "and the inevitable relaxation, or rather sinking of spirit, which follows violent mental exertion, are easily misconstrued into capricious rudeness, or intentional offence, and life is embittered by mutual accusation, not less intolerable because reciprocally unjust." Such were the difficulties under which the domestic peace both of Addison and Dryden went to wreck; and yet, say nothing of manners and habits of the highest elegance and polish in either case, they were both of them men of strictly pure and correct conduct in their conjugal capacities; and who can doubt that all these difficulties must have been enhanced tenfold, had any women of superior condition linked her fortunes with Robert Burns, a man at once of the very warmest animal tempera- ment, and the most wayward and moody of all his melancholy and irritable tribe, who had little vanity that could have been grateful by a species of con- nection, which, unless he had found a human angel, must have been continually wounding his pride? But, in truth, these speculations are all worse than worthless. Burns, with all his faults, was an honest and high-spirited man, and he loved the mother of his children; and had he hesitated to make her his wife, he must have sunk into the callousness of a ruffian, or that misery of miseries, the remorse of a poet.

The Reverend Hamilton Paul ("Life of Burns," p. 45) takes an original view of this business "Much praise," says he, "has been lavished on Burns for renewing his engagement with Jean when in the blaze of his fame. * * The praise is mis- placed. We do not think a man entitled to credit or commendation for doing what the law could compel him to perform. Burns was in reality a married man, and it is truly ludicrous to hear him, aware, as he must have been, of the indissoluble power of the obligation, though every document was destroyed, talking of himself as a bachelor."

To return to our story. Burns complains sadly of

solitary condition, when living in the only hovel that he found extant on his farm. "I am," says he (September 9th), "busy with my harvest; but for all that most pleasurable part of life called social intercourse, I am here at the very elbow of existence. The only things that are to be found in this country in any degree of perfection are stupidity and canting. Prose, they only know in graces, etc., and the value of these they estimate as they do their plaiding webs, by the ell. As for the Muses, they have as much idea of a rhinoceros as of a poet." And in a letter to Miss Chalmers (September 16th, 1788,) he says, "This hovel that I shelter in while occasionally here is pervious to every blast that blows, and every shower that falls, and I am only preserved from being chilled to death by being suffocated by smoke. You will be pleased to hear that I have laid aside idle eclat, and bind every day after my reapers."

His house, however, did not take much time in building, nor had he reason to complain of want of society long; nor, it must be added, did Burns bind every day after the reapers.

He brought his wife home to Ellisland about the end of November; and few housekeepers start with a larger provision of young mouths to feed than did this couple. Mrs. Burns had lain in this autumn, for the second time, of twins, and I suppose "sonsy, smirking, dear-bought Bess" accompanied her younger brothers and sisters from Mossgiel. From that quarter also Burns brought a whole establishment of servants, male and female, who, of course, as was then the universal custom amongst the small farmers, both of the west and south of Scotland, partook, at the same table, of the same fare with their master and mistress.

Ellisland is beautifully situated on the banks of the Nith, about six miles above Dumfries, exactly opposite to the house of Dalswinton, and those noble woods and gardens amidst which Burns's landlord, the ingenious Mr. Patrick Miller, found relaxation from the scientific studies and researches in which he so greatly excelled. On the Dalswinton side, the river washes lawns and groves: but over against these the bank rises into a long red scaut of considerable height, along the verge of which, where the bare shingle of the precipice all but overhangs the stream, Burns had his favourite walk, and might now be seen striding alone, early and late, especially when the winds were loud, and the waters below him swollen and turbulent. For he was one of those that enjoy nature most in the more serious and severe of her aspects; and throughout his poetry, for one allusion to the liveliness of spring, or the splendor of summer, it would be easy to point out twenty in which he records the solemn delight with which he contemplated the melancholy grandeur of autumn, or the savage gloom of winter. Indeed, I cannot but think, that the result of an exact inquiry into the composition of Burns's poems, would be, that "his vein," like that of Milton, flowed most happily "from the autumnal equinox to the vernal." Of Lord Byron, we know that his vein flowed best at midnight; and Burns has himself told us, that it was his custom "to take a gloamin' shot at the Muses."

The poet was accustomed to say, that the most happy period of his life was the first winter he spent at Ellisland, for the first time under a roof of his own, with his wife and children about him: and in spite of occasional lapses into the melancholy which had haunted his youth, looking forward to a life of

well-regulated, and not ill-rewarded, industry. It is
known that he welcomed his wife to her roof-tree at
Ellisland in the song,—

> "I hae a wife o' my ain, I'll partake wi' naebody;
> I'll tak cuckold frae nane, I'll gie cuckold to naebody.
> I hae a penny to spend—there, thanks to naebody;
> I hae nothing to lend—I'll borrow frae naebody."

In commenting on this "little lively lucky song,"
as he well calls it, Mr. Allan Cunningham says:
"Burns had built his house,—he had committed his
seed—corn to the ground,—he was in the prime, nay
the morning of life,—and strength, and agricultural
skill were on his side,—his genius had been
acknowledged by his country, and rewarded by a
subscription more extensive than any Scottish poet
ever received before; no wonder, therefore, that he
broke out into voluntary song, expressive of his
sense of importance and independance." Another
song was composed in honor of Mrs. Burns, during
the happy weeks that followed her arrival at
Ellisland:—

> "Oh, were I on Parnassus hill,
> Or had of Helicon my fill,
> That I might catch poetic skill,
>   To sing how dear I love thee!
>
> But Nith maun be my muse's well,
> My muse maun be thy bonnie sel',
> On Corsincon I'll glowre and spell,
>   And write how dear I love thee!"

MRS. BURNS' CIRCUMSTANCES AFTER THE POET'S DEATH.

The only dependence of Mrs. Burns, after her husband's death, was on an annuity of ten pounds, arising from a benefit society connected with the Excise, the books and other moveable property left to her, and the generosity of the public. The subscription, as we are informed by Dr. Currie, produced seven hundred pounds; and the works of the poet, as edited with regular taste and judgment by that gentleman, brought nearly two thousand more. One half of the latter sum was lent on a bond to a Galloway gentleman who continued to pay five per cent. for it till a late period. Mrs. Burns was thus enabled to support and educate her family in a manner creditable to the memory of her husband. She continued to reside in the house which had been occupied by her husband and herself, and

——" never changed, nor wished to change her place."

For many years after her sons had left her to pursue their fortunes in the world, she lived in a decent and respectable manner, on an income which never amounted to more than £62 per annum. At length, in 1817, at a festival held in Edinburgh to celebrate the birth-day of the bard, Mr. Henry, (now Lord) Cockburn acting as president, it was proposed by Mr. Maule of Panmure (now Lord Panmure), that some permanent addition should be made to the income of the poet's widow. The idea appeared to be favourably received, but the subscription did not fill rapidly. Mr. Maule then said that the burden of the provision should fall upon himself, and immediatcly executed a bond, entitling Mrs. Burns to an annuity of £50 as long as she lived. This act, together with the generosity of the same gentleman to Nathaniel Gow, in his latter and evil days, must ever endear the name of Lord Panmure to all who feel warmly on the subjects of Scottish poetry and Scottish music. Mr. Maule's pension had not been enjoyed by the widow more than a year and a half, when her youngest son, James, attained the rank of Captain with a situation in the commissariat, and was thus enabled to relieve her from the necessity of being beholden to a stranger's hand for any share of her support. She accordingly resigned the pension. Mr. M'Diarmid, who records these circumstances, adds in another place, that during her subsequent years, Mrs. Burns enjoyed an income of about two hundred a year, a great part of which, as it was not needed by her, she dispensed in charities. Her whole conduct in widowhood was such as to secure universal esteem in the town where she resided. She died March 26, 1834, in the 68th year of her age, and was buried beside her illustrious husband, in the mansoleum at Dumfries.

BONNIE JEAN.

By George Dobie.

We'll sing the nicht Jean Armour's praise,
　She's worthy o' a sang,
For it was Burns, her ain guidman,
　That raised her 'bin the thrang.
While bleechin' claes on Mauchline Braes,
　By Rab she first was seen,
Where Cupid's darts pierced baith the hearts
　O' Burns and bonnie Jean.

Jean was the jewel o' his heart,
　The apple o' his e'e,
And little kent that country maid
　That she a queen wad be.
For to us lang she'll reign in sang,
　And gain oor high esteem;
She prov'd through life a faithfu' wife,
　Our poet's bonnie Jean.

To Burns, Jean was the sweetest lass
　That ever graced the West,
Nae ither belle could her surpass,
　She was to him the best.
The westlin' win's will cease to blaw,
　And gowans deck the green,
Before it ever fades awa'
　The name o' bonnie Jean.

On this, the poet's natal day,
　We'll sing to bonnie Jean;
Had Rab himsel' been here to hear't,
　He had been proud, I ween.
For this ance charmin', artless lass,
　This peerless village queen,
She'll lang remembered be by us
　As Burn's bonnie Jean.

DEATH AND CHARACTER OF MRS. BURNS.

From Blackie's Edition of Burns.

At a late hour of the night of Wednesday, the 26th March, 1834, the world and its concerns closed forever on Mrs. Jean Armour,—the venerable relict of the Poet Burns. On the Saturday preceding, she was seized with paralysis for the fourth time during the last few years; and although perfectly conscious of her situation, and the presence of friends, became deprived, before she could be removed to bed, of the faculty of speech, and in a day or two thereafter of the sense of hearing. Still she lay wonderfully calm and composed, and, in the opinion of the medical attendant, suffered from weakness rather than from pain. Frequently she gazed, with the greatest earnestness, on her grand-daughter, Sarah; and it was easy to read what was passing within, from the tears that filled her aged eyes, and trickled down her cheeks. To another individual she directed looks so eager and full of meaning, as to impress him with the idea that she had some dying request to make, and deeply regretted that it was too late; for even if her salvation had depended on the exertion, she was unfortunately incapacitated from uttering a syllable, guiding a pen, or even making an intelligent sign. The mind, in her case, survived the body; and this, perhaps, was the only painful circumstances attending her death-bed,—considering how admirable her conduct had always been, her general health so sound, her span protracted beyond the common lot, her character for prudence and piety so well established, and her situation in life every way so comfortable. On the night of Tuesday, or morning of Wednesday, a fifth shock, unperceived by the attendants, deprived Mrs. Burns of mental consciousness; and from that time, till the hour of her death, her situation was exactly that of a breathing corpse. And thus passed away all that remained of " Bonnie Jean,"—the relict of a man, whose fame is as wide as the world itself, and the venerated heroine of many a lay which bid fair to live in the memories of the people of Scotland, and of thousands far removed from its shores, as long as the language in which they are written is spoken or understood.

The deceased was born at Mauchline, in February 1765, and thus entered the seventieth year of her age. Her father was an industrious master mason, in good employment, who enjoyed the esteem of the gentry and others within the district, and reared the numerous family of eleven sons and daughters, four of whom still survive,—viz: Robert, a respectable merchant in London; James, who resides in the town of Paisley; Mrs. Lees and Mrs. Brown. The alleged circumstances attending Mrs. Burns' union with the Bard are well known, and may be dismissed with the remark, that we have good authority for saying, that they have been incorrectly narrated by nearly every writer who has touched upon the subject. To the poet, Jean Armour bore a family of five sons and four daughters. The whole of the latter died in early life, and were interred in the cemetery of their maternal grandfather in Mauchline church-yard. Of the sons two died very young,—viz: Francis Wallace and Maxwell Burns, the last of whom was a posthumos child. born the very day his father was buried. Of the said family of nine three sons survive—Robert, the eldest, a retired officer of the Accomptant-General's Department, Stamp Office, London, now in Dumfries; and William and James Glencairn Burns, in the Hon. the East India Company's service.

Burns certainly left his family poor, (and how could it be otherwise?) but it is not true, as Collector Findlater has most successfully shown, that they were in immediate want, or lacked any necessary comfort. The relief fund annuity of an Exciseman's widow is known to be small (now, we believe about £12 per annum); but Providence, shortly after the husband and father's decease, raised up to the family many valuable friends. Passing exigencies were supplied from this honourable source; and no lengthened period elapsed until the active and disinterested benevolence of Dr. Currie, in conjunction with his excellent talents, placed at the feet of the family, to the great delight of the people of Scotland, very nearly £2,000 sterling, in name of profits arising from the Liverpool edition of the Poet's works. The Poet died in 1796, and up to 1818, his widow's income exceeded not, if it equalled, sixty pounds per annum. But on this sum, small as it may appear, she contrived to maintain a decent appearance, was never known to be in debt or wanting in charity—so unaspiring were her ambition and views, and undeviating her prudence, economy, and frugality. At the period just mentioned, Captain James Glencairn Burns wrote in breathless haste from India to say that having obtained promotion, through the kindness of the Marquis of Hastings, he had been enabled to set apart £150 yearly for the uses of his mother, and, as an earnest of affection, transmitted a draft for £75. And it is due to this gentleman to say, that from first to last, including some assistance from his brother, and allowances for his infant daughter, Sarah, he remitted his mother in all the handsome sum of £2,400 sterling. Leave of absence, and some other circumstances, at length impaired the means, and changed the fortunes, of the individual alluded to; Captain William Burns, later in life very cheerfully took his brother's place, and discharged, with equal promptitude, generosity, and affection, duties dear to the best and kindliest feelings of our nature. In this way, for sixteen years at the least, Mrs. Burns enjoyed an income of £200 per annum—a change of fortune which enabled her to add many comforts to her decent domicile, watch over the education of a favourite grandchild, and exercise, on a broader scale, the Christian duty of charity, which she did the more efficiently by acting in most cases as her own almoner.

It is generally known, that Mrs. Dunlop of Dunlop was the first efficient patroness of Robert Burns. Of the accuracy of this fact his writings furnish the most undoubted proof; and it would appear that her children inherited her feelings and spread the same mantle of friendship over the Poet's family. For a greater number of years than our memory can trace, Mrs. Burns dined every Sunday, after attending the divine service in St. Michael's Church, with the late Mrs. Perochan, the eldest daughter of Mrs. Dunlop of Dunlop; and was noticed and patronised in the most flattering manner by various living members of the same ancient family, who might feel offended did we dare to record all we happen to know of their exertions in a cause which Scotsmen, wherever situated, are prone to identify with the land of their birth.

The term of Mrs. Burns' widowhood extended to thirty-eight years, in itself rather an unusual circumstance—and in July 1796, when the bereavement occurred, she was but little beyond the age at which the majority of females marry. But she had too much respect for the memory of her husband, and regard for his children, to think of changing her name, although she might have done so more than once with advantage; and was even careful to secure on lease, and repair and embellish, as soon as she could afford it, the decent though modest mansion in which he died. And here, for more than thirty years, she was visited by thousands of strangers from the Peer down to itinerant sonneteers—a class of persons to whom she never refused an audience, or dismissed unrewarded. Occasionally, during the summer months, she was a good deal annoyed; but she bore all in patience, and although naturally fond of quiet, seemed to consider her house as open to visitors, and its mistress, in some degree, the property of the public. But the attentions of strangers neither turned her head, nor were ever alluded to in the spirit of boasting; and had it not been for a female friend who accompanied her on one occasion to the King's Arms Inn, to meet, by invitation, the Marchioness of Hastings, no one could have known that that excellent lady directed the present Marquis, who was then a boy, to present Mrs. Burns with a glass of wine, and at the same time remarked that "he should consider himself very highly honoured, and cherish the recollection of having met the Poet's widow, as long as he lived." Hers, in short, was one of those well-balanced minds that cling instinctively to propriety and the medium in all things; and such as knew the deceased, earliest and latest, were unconscious of any change in her demeanor and habits, excepting, perhaps, greater attention to dress, and more refinement of manner, insensibly acquired by frequent intercourse with families of the first respectability. In her tastes, she was frugal, simple, and pure; and delighted in music, pictures, and flowers. In spring and summer, it was impossible to pass her windows without being struck with the beauty of the floral treasures they contained; and if extravagant in anything, it was in the article of roots and plants of the finest sort. Fond of the society of young people, she mingled, as long as able, in their innocent pleasures, and cheerfully filled for them the cup " which cheers but not inebriates." Although neither a sentimentalist nor a " blue stocking," she was a clever woman, possessed great shrewdness, discriminated character admirably, and frequently made very pithy remarks; and were this the proper place for such detail proofs of what is stated might easily be adduced.

When young, she must have been a handsome comely woman, if not indeed a beauty, when the Poet saw her for the first time on a bleaching-green at Mauchline, engaged like Peggy and Jenny at Habbie's Howe. Her limbs were cast in the finest mould; and up to middle life her jet-black eyes were clear and sparkling, her carriage easy, and her step light. The writer of the present sketch never saw Mrs. Burns dance, nor heard her sing; but he has learned from others that she moved with great grace on the floor, and chanted her "wood-notes wild " in a style but rarely equalled by unprofessional singers. Her voice was a brilliant treble, and in singing "Coolen," "I gaed a waefu' gate yestreen," and other songs, she rose without effort as high as B natural. In ballad poetry her taste was good, and range of reading rather extensive. Her memory, too, was strong, and she could quote when she chose at considerable length, and with great aptitude.

Of these powers the bard was so well aware that he read to her almost every piece he composed, and was not ashamed to own that he had profited by her judgment. In fact, none save relations, neighbors, and friends, could form a proper estimate of the character of Mrs. Burns. In the presence of strangers she was shy and silent, and required to be drawn out, or, as some say, shown off to advantage, by persons who possessed her confidence, and knew her intimately.

But we have, perhaps, said enough, and although our heart has been thrown into our words, the portrait given is so strictly true to nature, that we conclude by saying, in the spirit of friendship, not of yesterday,—peace to the manes, and honour to the memory, of Bonnie Jean.

The remains of Mrs. Burns were interred in the family vault on Tuesday, the 1st April, with many marks of public respect, in presence of an immense crowd of spectators. Independently of the Bard's Mausoleum, St. Michael's Churchyard is perhaps the most remarkable cemetery in Britain; amidst innumerable tombs thousands on thousands sleep below; and on the day alluded to, public interest or curiosity waxed so intensely, that it became, if such an expression may be used, instinct with life as well as death. By many, a strong wish was expressed that the funeral should be made broadly public; others again objected to everything like parade, as unsuited to the quiet retiring character of the deceased; and amidst counsels and wishes so opposite and conflicting, the relatives and executors had a duty to discharge which was felt to be exceedingly onerous and perplexing. The Magistrates and Commissioners of Police politely offered to mark their respect for Mrs. Burns' memory by attending her funeral in their public capacity—an offer so honourable that it was at once acknowledged and acceded to by the trustees. But something more was wanted, in the opinion of at least a portion of the public; and as the street in which the deceased resided is short, narrow and situated so near to the churchyard, as to injure the appearance of the procession, it was anxiously asked that the coffin should be conveyed in a hearse to the Council Chambers stairs, and from thence carried shoulder-high along the line of the principal street. On reflection, however, it was deemed better that the living should go to the dead, than the dead to the living The Magistrates agreed in the propriety of this, and issued cards to the whole of the Council, appointing a meeting at half-past eleven on the morning of Tuesday, at which hour they assembled, and shortly after moved in a body to Burns' street, amidst a throng of people, many of whom had voluntarily arrayed themselves in sables such as has rarely been witnessed on the streets of Dumfries. Between two and three hundred funeral letters were issued in compliance with the usual custom; and in this way, while the private feeling of friends were conciliated, the public were gratified in as far as was deemed consistent with the rules of decorum.

As many persons were received into the house as it could possibly contain, including various clergymen, citizen friends, and country gentlemen, among the latter of whom we observed Sir Thos. Wallace, a kind personal friend of the deceased; Sir Thos. Kirkpatrick; Mr. Dunlop, Southwick; Mr. Jas. M'Alpine Leny of Dalswinton; Mr. John Dunlop, Rosefield; Mr. MacAdam, of Castledykes; Major Adair; Mr. Hannah, of Hannahfield; Major Davis; Mr. John Staig; the Provost and Magistrates, &c.,

&c. Eloquent prayers were put upon the occasion by the Reverend Messrs Wrightman, Fyffe, Dunlop, and Wallace; and after the usual forms had been observed, the coffin was placed on spokes, and borne by many to its final resting place. Throwing a stone to a chieftain's cairn was deemed an honour by our Celtic ancestors, and a similar feeling obviously prevailed in regard to the funeral obsequies of the Poet's widow. Before one person had well touched a spoke he was succeeded by another, eager to share in the same mournful duty; and although the distance was extremely short, several hundred hands bore the body along by shifting as frequently as St. Michael's bell tolled. Though the crowd was very dense, forests of heads were thrown into line as the procession moved forward; every window was filled with spectators; numerous visitors were observed from the country; and altogether, the scene reminded many of the memorable day of the Poet's funeral. So great was the anxiety to enter the Mausoleum, that the pressure, in the first instance, occasioned a slight degree of confusion; but in a minute or two order was restored, and the body lowered slowly and solemnly into the family vault. The chief mourners then descended, took the stations assigned to them, and after everything had been adjusted, placed the coffin in a grave dug to the depth of four feet. Five relatives attended the interment, viz, Mr. Robert Burns, eldest son of the Poet, Mr. Robert Armour, the widow's brother, and the husbands of three nieces, the Messrs Irving and Mr. M'Kinnel. But there were other chief mourners, and among those we observed Mr. Dunlop, of Southwick, Provost Murray, Dr. John Symons, Mr. Bogie, and Mr. M'Diarmid. The grave was covered in a brief space; the chief mourners then withdrew; and after every thing foreign had been removed from the vault, the executors gave the necessary directions for restoring the large stone which guards the entrance to the tomb of our great national poet. As this was a task of considerable labour, hours elapsed before it could be completed, and, in the interim, thousands had an opportunity of gratifying their curiosity by taking a parting look at the resting place of genius.

BRAVE BONNIE JEAN.

By Hon. Wallace Bruce.

" Brave Bonnie Jean!" we love to tell
  The story from thy lips that fell;
The lengthened life which Heaven gave.
  Casts radiant twilight on his grave.

A noble woman, strong to shield;
  Her tender heart his trusty bield;
The critic from her door-way turns
  With faith renewed and love for Burns.

She knew as no one else could know
  The heavy burden of his woe;
The carking care, the wasting pain—
  Each welded link of misery's chain.

She saw his early sky o'ercast,
  And gloomy shadows gathering fast;
His soul by bitter sorrow torn,
  And knew that " man was made to mourn."

She heard him by the sounding shore
  Which speaks his name for evermore,
And felt the anguish of his prayer:
  " Farewell, the bonnie banks of Ayr."

"OF A' THE AIRTS."

By Robert Ford.

Author of " Thistledown," " American Humorists," etc.

No song of Burns' has enjoyed greater public favor or will likely outlast in popularity this, one of the sweetest and most impassioned of all his glorious love lyrics. It was written in the midsummer of the year 1788, just when the poet had taken possession of the farm of Ellisland, in Dumfries-shire, and was overseeing the erection of a new farm-house and offices there, previous to the reception of Jean Armour as his legalized wife. His own note to it is simply this: "The air is by Marshall; the song I composed out of compliment to Mrs. Burns. *N. B.* —It was during the honeymoon." Earlier in the same year he sent a fragment of song—" My Jean " —to Johnson's *Museum*, and that is worth quoting here. There is only one verse:—

> Tho' cruel fate should bid us part,
>   Far as the pole and line—
> Her dear idea round my heart
>   Should tenderly entwine.
> Tho' mountains rise and deserts howl,
>   And oceans roar between—
> Yet, dearer than my deathless soul,
>   I still would love my Jean.

In these ruder, but not less impassioned, lines we discover the germ of the perfect lyric under comment. From the figure—

> Tho' mountains rise and deserts howl,
>   And oceans roar between.

the step in improvement is brief to—

> There's wild woods grows and rivers row,
> And mony a hill between.

And what follows these lines in either verse is not dissimilar in sentiment. The exact date of the song —"Of a' the Airts"—was presumably betwixt the 12th and 22nd of June, while the poet was in his solitude on the banks of the Nith, and his Bonnie Jean was at Mossgiel—to quote his own words—"regularly and constantly apprenticed to my mother and sister in their dairy and other rural business," for about this time also he represents his favorite mare, "Jenny Geddes," as being homesick:—

> Jenny, my Pegascan pride,
> Dowie she saunters down Nithside,
> And aye a westlan' leuk she throws,
> While tears hap o'er her auld brown nose.

The poet, too, is casting longing looks in the "westlan'," or, more strictly speaking, "north-westlan' airt," and his cry is—

> Of a' the airts the win' can blaw,
> I dearly like the west.

But the song itself:—

OF A' THE AIRTS.

> "Of a' the airts the wind can blaw,
>   I dearly like the west ;
> For there the bonnie lassie lives,
>   The lassie I lo'e best ;
> There's wild woods grow, and rivers row,
>   And mony a hill between ;
> But day and night my fancy's flight
>   Is ever wi' my Jean.

I see her in the dewy flowers,
  I see her sweet and fair :
I see her in the tunefu' birds,
  I hear her charm the air ;
There's not a bonnie flower, that springs,
  By fountain, shaw, or green ;
There's not a bonnie bird that sings,
  But minds me o' my Jean."

That is the song exactly as Burns wrote it; though, in all the song-collections, other verses are added, and even these are differently phrased. Some editors, in bad taste, have printed "lo'e" in the second line instead of "like," and nearly all have written—

Though wild woods grow and rivers row,
  Wi' mony a hill between.

With the second double stanza, still greater liberty has been taken; but, I think, to the improvement of the song. Let the reader compare the above with the following:—

I see her in the dewy flower,
  Sae lovely, sweet, and fair—
I hear her voice in ilka bird,
  Wi' music charm the air ;
There's not a bonnie flower that springs,
  By fountain, shaw, or green,—
Nor yet a bonnie bird that sings,
  But minds me o' my Jean.

The briefness of the song, too, hás tempted some respectable versifiers to make additions to it, for the sixteen lines of the text just go once through the melody. Mr. William Reid, a late bookseller in Glasgow—an inveterate song-tinker, who tried his hand on the "Lass o' Gowrie" and other popular measures—attempted a continuation. But Reid's lines, though frequently printed, are never sung. They are these:—

Upon the banks o' flowing Clyde
  The lasses busk them braw ;
But when their best they ha'e put on
  My Jeanie dings them a'.
In hamely weeds she far exceeds
  The fairest o' the town—
Baith sage and gay confess it sae,
  Though drest in russet gown.

The gamesome lamb, that sucks its dam,
  Mair harmless canna be ;
She has nae faut, if sic ye ca't,
  Except her love for me.
The sparkling dew, o' clearest hue,
  Is like her shining e'en—
In shape and air, wha can compare
  Wi' my sweet, lovely Jean.

Mr. John Hamilton of Edinburgh, author of " Up
in the Morning Early," next made the attempt, and
with much more success. His verses, in tenderness
of feeling and beauty of imagery, are not inferior to
those of Burns, although they may contain anachronisms, as Mr. Scott Douglas not unreasonably
avers. Hamilton's addition, which is invariably
sung, is as follows :—

O blaw, ye westlan' winds, blaw saft,
  Amang the leafy trees—
Wi' gentle gale, frae muir and dale,
  Bring hame the laden bees ;
And bring the lassie back to me
  That's aye sae neat and clean :
A'e blink o' her wad banish care,
  Sae lovely is my Jean.

What sighs and vows, amang the knowes,
  Ha'e pass'd atween us twa !
How fain to meet, how wae to part,
  That day she gaed awa !
The Powers aboon can only ken,
  To whom the heart is seen,
That nane can be sae dear to me,
  As my sweet, lovely Jean.

These verses, says Mr. Scott Douglas, are very musical and expressive; but were, unfortunately, composed under the mistaken idea that the absence of Jean, referred to in Burns' song, was that of Spring, 1786, when she removed to Paisley to avoid him. On the poet's own authority, however, the date and the occasion of the song are rendered certain, and, at that time, instead of imploring the west winds to "bring the lassie back" to him, he had only to return to *her;* and, moreover, she could not come "back" to Ellisland, where she had never yet been.

Notwithstanding these anachronisms, it is no small compliment to Mr. Hamilton that Burns' own sixteen lines are now seldom dissociated from his imitator's supplementary ones. Cunningham boldly tells his readers that the whole thirty-two lines are from Burns' own mannscript; Lockhart quotes the added lines as the poet's own; and Professor Wilson, in his famous "Essay," adopts Hamilton's addendum as an authentic part of the song. Its only weak line is—

> That's aye sae neat and clean—

which is not poetical at all, and might read—

> Wi' her twa witchin' een—

which is at once the language of love and poetry, and runs on a line with the rest of the sentiment.

JEAN ARMOUR.

A CHARACTER STUDY.

By The Rev. William Lowestofft.

Among all the women who crossed the path of Robert Burns, among all those whom he singled out for the bestowal of his affection, among all those to whom he poured out the accents of love, no one stands out in bolder relief for having won the victory over his wayward heart than does Jean Armour. We say this with as full a knowledge of his life as more or less constant and diligent study and enquiry can give; we say it with as clear a realization of the Clarinda interlude as it seems the facts warrant and with a more or less close study of the passages of which so many women in turn figured as the heroines. In his relation with "the sex" Robert Burns was not by any means a model of constancy. He soon tired of each succeeding flame and was ever eager to bask in new smiles. Having won a heart he seemed satisfied with victory and desired to add to his conquests and to his reputation as a gallant. No poet of whom we read, certainly no Scottish poet, had the lines of his life so often crossed by feminine charms, had the events of his career so shaped that through it all a woman starts up in one way or another as a controlling or degrading influence, and yet, when we review that life story, laying aside mere frivolities and gallantries and platonic friendships and paltry bits of romance, and more or less conventional extravagances of demeanor, we are forced to believe that there were but two women during the thirty-seven years of his life who completely held his heart and in their respective spheres reigned supreme—the mother whom he revered and the wife he loved.

We say this, too, with a full knowledge of his sins against the moral law and the consequences thereof. These sins we cannot condone and the time for explanation and consideration has passed. The green grass has long waved over the Jenny Clows and Betty Parks and their offspring and they have long passed away from the judgments of men. Nor would we even refer to them here but for the fact that such acquaintances, such intimacies, had a more or less direct influence on the heart of the poet, and had more or less to do with shaping his career. But we do not believe they gave him more than a passing thought, or had any influence whatever on his song. They undoubtedly did not elevate his ideas of human nature, especially female nature, nor did they enhance his sense of the dignity of the sex. But he was not foolish enough to believe from his knowledge of evil that all women were bad—that all were Jenny Clows. His knowledge of the weakness of the bad, the frail, the fallen, seemed rather to increase his admiration for the good and in that category, in spite of what had passed, he never failed to place—even in the dreary days of 1786—she who had trusted him to her sorrow, she who afterwards became his acknowledged and lawful wife.

And we also say this with a full study of the Highland Mary mystery—of the girl whom so many believe to be the real heroine of Burns's life, to whom in recognition of that sentiment many admirers—more or less silly—have erected a monument on the banks of the Clyde. Many writers of Burns's life have pretty fairly settled that Mary Campbell was a dairy-maid at Coilsfield and afterward a servant in the household of Gavin Hamilton, but others say she was not and are in doubt as to what she really was, Most of them describe her as a paragon of innocent virtue, some, however, more or less definately express doubt on that point. Burns's story is really all that we have on which to base our knowledge of the girl, and that story is so contradictory and so full of inconsistencies that we would throw it aside alto-gether as a myth, were it not for the presence of the Bible which remains as a witness of the actuality of the love passages in the graceful monument on the banks of the Doon.

But take it anyway we may, and we have viewed the matter from every conceivable standpoint, we cannot regard the Highland Mary incident as any other than simply one of the love passages in which the poet was engaged through his earlier life and into each of which he threw himself with all the in-tensity of his nature. He would have given Mary at the moment a stack of Bibles if she had asked for them and he had them to give, if thereby he could have proved the honesty of his intentions—for honest we believe him—for the time—to have been in all such intervals. We believe Mary very sincere in her love, and that she went from Ayrshire to her parents' home to prepare for her marriage. We do not believe that any woman ever lived, with the ex-ception of Clarinda, to whose heart the poet ever made siege who did not confess herself conquered, and even Clarinda was only retained from giving her hand and pledging her troth, by the knowledge that the law had set up a barrier between them which only death could sever. We see no reason for doubt-ing that Mary gave up her whole heart to Burns, but as for him, judging by his own record, she was no sooner out of his sight than he turned to bask in the sunshine of new smiles. Her sudden death brought her memory back again with irresistible force, but it was in reality that sudden death which made her memory immortal. The songs in which Burns has given her fame did not appear until long after, when all that was earthly in his passion had been purified by time, and her memory had been enhanced, etherialized, softened, and refined by absence, by a knowledge that she had passed from mortality and taken on the robes of immortality. But we cannot concede that Mary had any real influence on Robert Burns; so far as that was concerned she was little better than a lay figure in an artist's studio—the lay figure on which he drapes his costume and experiments with positions, and we do not doubt that the. real figure which suggested the many songs—the real inspirer of the lyrics which have made her rank as a heroine of Scottish songs was his own wife, the one being who gave him any practical happiness in the meridian and gloaming of life, Jean Armour.

On the surface there is little to tell of the life of " Bonnie Jean," as Jean Armour will be called until the art of love making is forgotten. She was born at Mauchline in 1765, was noted for her good looks, her shapely figure and sprightly conversation, was married to Robert Burns, whether in 1786 or 1788 does not matter here, bore him many children, survived him in widowhood for thirty-eight years and died in 1834 respected for her own sake, honored for the name she bore, and famous for the songs which had been written in her praise.

Not much to write about truly, not more than could be said of millions of women, except for the last clause in the above paragraph, who have lived

and died in the land of Robert Burns. Like them, too,
she would have been content to have remained forgotten after the darkness set in. But the pre-eminence
which he by his genius bestowed on all his kith and
kin, aye even on all in more or less degree who
crossed his pathway or journeyed with him even a
short distance along the highway of life, has placed
her on a pedestal and forced her into our thoughts.
Her life has been studied by the enthusiasts and
everything gleaned concerning her outgoings and
incomings which it was possible for diligent enquiry
—prurient as often as anything else—has been
placed before us and we are able, as a result to get
some sort of an idea of her character and of the
amiable qualities of head and heart, which, as well
as her personal charms, won for her the heart of
the greatest of Scotia's bards.

The story of that life is not without deep
significance for women. Jean Armour, somehow
the world does not seem to take kindly to the more
formal designation of Mrs. Burns, was by no means
a woman with a mission, she would have shrunk
with native delicacy from even remote association
with the shrieking sisterhood—the short haired
women who in the company of long haired men are
bellowing about the equality of the sexes and trying
to bring about some new sort of an era—all in five
minutes—on the face of the globe. But unconsciously
she had a mission, and unconsciously her memory
pleads in one respect at least for equality for her
sisters with the sterner sex.

In the usual acceptance of the world Jean " fell "
before any form of marriage ceremony passed between her and the poet. According to the general
theory this involved her moral ruin, and upset any
idea that might be entertained of her possessing any

regard for virtue, of her being aught but a wanton. The certificate which she obtained from her lover, a sort of acknowledgment of her as his wife, did not alter the state of the case at all or even atone for the sin. Under such circumstances a young woman generally finds that her entire character is gone, her future life blasted, and the finger of levity or scorn is pointed at her, while the arm of the libertine is ever ready to encircle her and draw her still further from the moral highway. Whoever has read—and who has not?—Hawthorne's magnificent study "The Scarlet Letter" can understand readily all that we mean, all that we imply in these lines. The world looked darkly at her; even her own people rebelled against her unjustly and her prudish sisters cast reproachful glances at her as she passed. Defiantly the author of her misfortune wrote about the same time:

> Ye high exalted, virtuous dames
> Ty'd up in godly laces,
> Before ye gie poor Frailty names
> Suppose a change of places,
> A dear-lov'd lad, convenience snug
> A treacherous inclination,
> But let me whisper in your lug
> Ye're ailbins nae temptation.
>
> Then gently scan your brother man,
> Still gentler sister woman ;
> Tho' they may gang a kennin' wrang
> To step aside is human,
> One point must still be greatly dark
> The moving *why* they do it,
> And just as lanely can ye mark
> How far perhaps they rue it.

It is commonly argued, and whether argued or not it is commonly held, that when a woman "makes a slip" as the saying goes—she is bound to fall beyond hope of recovery. Legally Jean Armour fell. She broke the laws of both kirk and state, but who with a knowledge of her life can ever accuse her of being an immoral woman, of being aught but a pure, trusting, loving heart. Did she even under the circumstances violate a moral law? That is a question we have often asked ourselves and been unable to clearly answer in the affirmative.

Be it understood we are not condoning or defending wantonness or licentiousness. We do not believe there is a more loathsome sight in the world than a wanton, licentious woman, but who with a knowledge of Jean Armour's life can place such accusations at her door. Nay, we go further in our defence of her position in the evil days of 1786 and say that we believe that morally she never fell at all but that, trusting to her chosen lover, she accepted his promises, his protestations, blindly and impassionately, and that while she broke the laws by which society is regulated. she broke them not because she was a wanton, but because as a woman with a wooer like Robert Burns she could not help herself.

So we take it that a mission might be cut out for Jean Armour and that mission might be stated to be an equality of the sexes as regards the condonation of moral wrongs. Her long, and but for this incident morally blameless life, her fidelity to her husband—a fidelity which was not reciprocal and of which the "misfortune" of Annie Park was, we fear only one instance. Remember in this we are not trying to show the poet's guilt—there is no use considering this—it is all past and gone—but we merely bring up a perfectly reliable and acknowledged instance to prove that Jean preserved the moral amenities when her own husband showed, without any attempt apparently at concealment, that the vows of matrimony did not circumscribe his conduct or be to him a moral shield. But Jean was loyal to Burns from the day she met him first, whether when bleaching claes on the green at Mauchline or at a penny wedding, until her body was laid beside his in the mansoleum which his countrymen, his admirers, had erected in auld St. Michael's Churchyard to guard his honored dust.

Jean Armour loved the poet from the first with all the love which a woman can give a man, during their married life at Ellisland and in "the Dark Days of Dumfries." In spite of trials and offences not one or two, but oft repeated, offences which would try, which have tried and broken, the temper, the fidelity, the love, even the character of thousands of women, she still held to her love, condoned his offenses, thought as lightly as was possible over his transgressions and did what she could to "make a happy fireside clime." So far as we have read no word of reproach ever escaped her lips, she did not storm, or rave, at faults or follies, at the idea of facing poverty, at seeing the family fortunes steadily going down, nor did she lose heart when it was seen that the end was surely coming and her husband was entering on that contest in which all must surrender —the contest with the grim conqueror. Her love, her faith, in his genuine goodness never wavered and when critics and biographers and literary hyenas of all sorts were hounding his memory, raking up all the gossip—vile and paltry and generally exaggerated if not altogether untrue—which the "clash" of a country town can furnish, her voice was never uttered but in praise, and his conduct as a husband and father elicited from her nothing but words of grateful commendation. She understood her husband better than did the critics and hyenas and knew what he had to contend against—physically and mentally, better than they and was able to give a clearer opinion as to his moral worth. She understood clearer than they the full import of the bard's lines in the poem from which we have already quoted:

> "Who made the heart, 'tis He alone
>   Decidedly can try us;
> He knows each chord its various tone,
>   Each spring its various bias.
> Then at the balance let's be mute
>   We never can adjust it,
> What's done we partly may compute,
>   But know not what's resisted."

Then her long blameless widowhood, her humble yet wholly successful effort to bring up her family so that they might make their way in the world to higher social spheres than that in which she had moved, her regard for the reputation of the bard, her constant work of charity, her religious faith, all point to her as a woman in whom the beauty of the moral law was conspicuous. She observed all the proprieties of life, she circumscribed her conduct so that not a whisper could be raised even by envy— and all little country towns are full of that—and she earned, well earned, the reputation of being a good woman, a lovable woman, a charitable woman, one who was constantly, daily, engaged in laying up treasures in heaven.

And yet, once, she had what the world called fallen, and the finger of scorn was pointed at her for her offence. Surely if an erring woman desires to retain hope, desires to understand how it is possible to outlive a fault, how it is possible for a woman to be led into folly and yet retain her own self respect and by her own behavior make even the world condone or forget her error, she can find not only an example, but an influence in thinking over the career of Bonnie Jean and recalling the glorious golden sunset of life after a gloomy spring time. Rightly understood, we take it, Jean Armour, while not a woman with a mission, did actually perform a mission and left a legacy to her sisters, as important, as full of hope, as comforting in its way as that which her gifted husband left to mankind.

There is another phase in which the career of Jean Armour is of deep interest and that is in its unconscious intellectual growth. In this respect in fact, she is a representative type of her country-women in her own rank of life and a type which still exists even although education is much more thorough a factor in the county districts of Scotland than it was in her girlhood days. Practically she was un-educated. She could read a little, very little. It is doubtful if she could write. She was not, in early life at all events, at all fond even of what we call improving the mind. Yet she had a retentive mem-ory, a sweet voice, a native shrewdness and a degree of quick-wittedness which enabled her to readily understand whatever subject was discussed in her presence and to appreciate her own shortcoming. She knew all the legends of the countryside in which she had her home, she was aquainted with the words and airs of every scrap of song and ballad which floated around the village, and her ability as a dancer gave her a carriage and a presence which, in addition to her good looks, captured more hearts than that of Rob Mossgiel. The manufacture of rhyme, the technicalities of feet and measure were to her mysteries as profound, if not more so than those of a mason's lodge, and yet when her husband wanted the voice of an honest critic over some piece of literary work he submitted the production to her judgment and invariably profited by it. Her practical ideas were a good antidote to his theoretical notions. He said himself "If I have not got polite tattle, modish manners and fashionable dress, I am not sickened and disgusted with the multiform curse of boarding school affectation. I have got the handsomest figure, the sweetest temper, the soundest constitution and the kindest heart in the country."

Doubtless from the time she went to Ellisland and became mistress of her own home Jean's character mellowed, her knowledge of the world around her widened and her opportunities for mental improvement increased and she took full advantage of her position. We do not learn that she devoted herself to books, indeed we have evidence that her one book was the Bible, with now and then, perhaps, a glance through some volume bearing her husband's name. But most of his songs she knew by heart and when she sung them, or crooned them over as she went about her household duties she delighted his heart more than though her voice had been that of the most accomplished prima donna, because, somehow, in her singing she evolved the very sentiment, the pith, the full meaning of the song.

To the end of her career, Jean Armour owned nothing intellectually to books, yet who would, even in these modern days describe her as an ignorant woman. Her tact enabled her to conceal her shortcomings, her manner threw in the background any mistake in speech she might make, any misunderstanding of a particular subject, and any little break of etiquette of which she might be guilty. No one of course could be associated with Burns and not feel the influence of his genius, and we almost fancy that Jean with a woman's adaptability soon acquired his sense of taste in poetry, his aspirations for good

—and rejected with her finer instincts and purer ideas all that was gross and earthly. Her retentive memory gave her the mastery of any subject which was once discussed in her presence, her clear perception of right and wrong led her to a just decision on any topic and her shrewd common sense supplied the rest.

During her long widowhood her home was invaded by inquisitive strangers of all sorts, some on errands which commanded her sympathy, others with missions which, as they related to her husband's memory required all her tact, and others whose only purpose was idle curiosity and who filled her with contempt —contempt which however she rarely showed. These visitors were of all classes and conditions of men and women, and their conversation naturally ranged from technical to commonplace, and yet we cannot recall one instance when a visitor has left on record any impressisn that he regarded Jean Armour as an ignorant woman. She met her visitors on their own level, apparently without effort, without affection, and charmed them all. The Marchioness of Hastings, not only was delighted with her, but told her son to remember the interview with Mrs. Burns as an honor,—which he did. The landed gentry were interested in her and she met them on an even footing, whether they came to her home or she met them accidently as she moved through the streets of Dumfries. Every clergyman in the town held her in the highest esteem and none regarded her as a woman whose education had been neglected or one to whom it was necessary to "speak down to her level" as the professional phrase goes. Of her husband she spoke without extravagance, defending his memory in her quiet but effective way from its detractors great and small; of her family she was

proud and she saw them—or some of them—make
their way in the world in a manner that would have delighted their father—winning praises on all sides for
their good qualities, and giving her substantial
evidence of their reverence and their love.

A country girl without book learning, a widowed
matron, mingling we might say in all classes and
" keeping up her own end " in any conversation, in
any society, can we consider the widow of Robert
Burns an ignorant woman? Surely not. Her life
shows that even the three r's are, after all but a
foundation, and that with native wit, by taking advantage of all other opportunities, a superstructure
of knowledge may be raised without their aid. True
the superstructure is not so solid as it might be with
their help; true, the absence of their aid is to be ever
deplored, but if we can learn anything from Jean
Armour's career it is that their aid is not indispens-
able to the sphere in which the poet's wife, in poverty
or affluence, confined herself—that of a busy, kindly
country housewife. She would not have been any
better for having had the foundation, she might with
it and reached into realms of which she had no ken,
but she supplied their want by her own wit and
probably when she died had a fund of knowledge
equal to any woman of her class in the three
kingdoms.

At times we hear men being rated as uneducated
if they have not passed, no matter how slovenly,
through a college curriculum, and a young woman
is still spoken of as uneducated if she cannot work
out a problem of Euclid or construe a few lines
from Thucydides. To be "educated" she must
speak French—or be able to make a bluff at it—turn
out wonderful effects in ribbon and lace and paint—
heaven save the mark—jars and jugs and crockery

of all sorts. No matter if the man thus blessed knows at the end of his career little more than to kick a football, or the girl barely enough to cement a bit of crystal. They are "educated." However, a new era is dawning and education—as simply a preparation for life is being better understood and the boy or girl graduating from the Grammar school, if they but use the foundation then acquired aright can force the world to acknowledge them as being educated men and women.

So Jean Armour, with no deeper foundation than that which permitted her in early life to read her Bible, passed through her long career not only without calling attention to her lack of "book learning" but with the reputation for being the very reverse of ignorant. We do not despise education, far from it, but the story of Jean Armour illustrates one fact often—invariably—overlooked—that primary education is simply a means to an end, and that end, can be reached by the exercise of that art, shrewdness, and natural curiosity which are our heritage from nature.

TO ROBERT BURNS.

By Dr. Benjamin F. Leggett.

O peasant Bard whose sweet voice stirs
   The heather of the hills;
How far and wide thy song has flown—
   How every measure thrills!

Thy name is dear to Scotia's land,
   She will not let it die:
The daisy prints it on the ground,—
   The laverock on the sky.

The cottar in his ingle-neuk,
   The gowan on the brae,
They keep thy fame so tenderly
   It cannot pass away.

Not less of tender love for thee,
   Holds every heart that turns,
To greet, with loyal homage due,
   Thy Bonnie Jean,—O Burns!

Her eyes for thee held starry hope
   To cheer thy darkest dream,—
With light she filled thy humble home—
   The light of love supreme.

Thou hast no need of measured line
   To keep thy memory green;—
One sang for loyal womanhood—
   Thy guid wife—Bonnie Jean!

THE POET AND HIS WIFE.

By Rev. Arthur John Lockhart.
"Pastor Felix."

As we ask again for the singing of some old song, which has gathered to its perfect heart the loves and joys and sorrows of a hundred generations; or, as we listen again to the telling of some sweet story that makes its unchanging appeal to our affections, though rehearsed a thousand times, while the familiar recital "wearies not ever;"—so we are never tired of listening to the romantic, yet deeply-human, history of Robert Burns,—who, in the heart's matters, is "all mankind's epitome." Currie may tell it, and we are no less ready to listen to Cunningham; Lockhart's recital but whets our appetite for Carlyle; we rise up from Professor Nichol or Robert Chambers to sit down expectant and eager when the next one is ready to tell the story in his own way. The spirits of envy and disapprobation seem half disarmed; and we grudge our praise no more than we do our smiles when some lovely child has come within the sphere of our vision.

Burns was more than a poet potentially, but one by actual and noble accomplishment, before he met the woman of whom he could say,—"my Jean,"—the companion of his few bitter years—the drop of wine and honey in his gall; but Scotland and the world did not yet know it,—only the little world of his intimates at Mossgiel, at Mauchline and Tarbolton. The buds of song had been folded in the babe at Alloway, but they were now buds no longer. The wild rose hedges on Doon's green banks are not more full of birds and blossoms in their time than was his heart with broad-blown melodies; and some of the sweetest the world will not let die had already been scrawled by that heavy hand, furtively and hastily, in that rough garret at Lochlea, and hidden in the deal desk. He was not like some of us, who have to sit on a green bank by a running stream and dream we are poets,—never ceasing to wish we could be, and trying again and again to persuade ourselves and the world that we are, while the world will not heed us, and, for the most part, we doubt ourselves. He rose up, half in a maze of wonder, shook his locks, and without speculation, put forth power. The harp of Scotland was not hung up out of his reach; and when he took it down he did not pick a random chord with hap-hazard fingers, but swept them all like the master he was; the listeners were all thrilled as he plucked a living soul out of every wire. With what grace Raphæl painted and Mozart composed, with the like grace Burns gave us his memorable poesy. Long ago he had tasted love, and knew its sweetness and its sharpness, its power to "wreck his peace," and to renew its enchantment, as charmer after charmer passed before him. Love and music consented together with him, and the genius of his life appeared in company with "lovely Nell," and setting suns, and autumnal moonlight in the barley-field.

Jean Armour rose, a star above the cloudy days at Mossgiel; and, though she disappeared again for a season, she emerged low on the horizon of home, where she lingered; and only by the wrack of death that enveloped him was he ever again bereaved of her presence. Let us recur to the pleasant story of their first meeting. A Scottish merry-making, as the poet tells us, was often the scene where that soft

flame, which may burn well or ill, has its beginning.
It was at such a one, when Mauchline fair was held,
that the die was cast for him. On the race day the
house of entertainment became an open court of
pleasure, and he who would freely came with his
favorite lass, without cost, withal,—unless it be the
cost of his heart, and a penny contribution to the
fiddler. Burns came that day, with his companion,
who hung not on his arm, but ran at his heels.
When I read Joanna Baillie's song,—

> " Saw ye Johnnie comin' ? said she ;
> " Saw ye Johnnie comin' ?
> Wi' his blue bonnet on his head
> And his doggie rinnin',—

I think of lonesome Robin, with his dumb and over-
fond companion. But Jean was there, with eyes
already bent upon him, and ears quickened at his
words. Though old father Armour will listen un-
moved to the song's petition—

> " Fee him, faither, fee him,"

yet the heart of a woman goeth whither it will, and,
while her lips protest, her look surrenders. Robert's
dog at his heels through the round of every dance,
became the occasion of some mirthful glances and
some poking of fun at the poet, to whose proud
spirit even such light banter was never very agreeable. But he, who was never behindhand with his
rejoinder, expressed a wish that he could find in some
lassie his dog's peer in affectionate fidelity,—a wish
Jean overheard, and which in her heart, perhaps
at a later time, she determined to gratify.

If there is a romantic attractiveness in the story
of the poet's meeting with Highland Mary on that

blissful day in Montgomerie's woods,—an attractiveness like that of the old ballad, made we know not
by whom,—

> " When shaws beene sheene, and shradds full fayre,
> And leeves both large and longe ;—

there is likewise a beguiling touch of homely poetry,
befitting Jean Armour's character, in his next meeting with her, only a day or two after the evening at
the inn at Mauchline, where—

> " To the trembling string
> The dance gaed thro' the lighted ha' ;"

and where, though we are told she did not join with
him, we would not dare to pronounce her averse to
it. The summer air breathed on her sweet cheek as
she stood on the green where her linen lay bleaching, and the summer sunlight fell on her fine brow
and fair locks, when along came Robin from the
riverside, gun in hand,—to find game no such
weapon could bring down. The hare, and the
mousie, and the water-fowl on Loch Turit, having
nothing to fear, the lassies, that may be slain by
arrows from the bow of his eyes, may beware
accordingly. If Robert is in dowie mood he sud-
denly gladdens at the sight of the sonsie brunette,
and thanks his dog for a confab, and a chance to
stand at gaze. Jean is not inclined to allow dirty
tracks on her clean linen, and is petulant as any nice
house-body might be at the prospect of such defile-
ment. So doggie gets a stone hurled at his head,
and his owner hears a peremptory summons to call
him off. But when the poet draws near, and she
comes under the spell of that tongue so like "a
silver lute," her look and tone soften, and she slyly
asks him if yet he had found a lass to love him.

Then, I can think, these words had pathos: "Lassie, if ye thocht ocht o' me, ye wadna hurt my dog." Jean's unspoken comment,—"I wadna think much o' you, at ony rate,"—must have belied her heart. It was the hasty defiance from the commander of a poorly garrisoned fortress on the evening before surrender.

Now soon can that hopeful and gratified lover break out in song over the daughter of the master mason of Mauchline,—

> "A dancin', sweet, young handsome queen
>   Of guileless heart."

Alas, for Jean! who surrendered too easily, and returned the poet's love with too much abandon; better had she been frugal, where he was so lavish, to reserve her gifts. Too soon for both of them did "sweet affection prove the spring of woe." In brief time the lassie lets tears fall upon her pillow, and Robin has a secret in his breast he "daurna tell to ony,"—nay, will not even venture to whisper to the muse, so ready to condone our faults and compassionate our sorrows. But the day of revealment must come, and the blush burn the cheek of mother and sister, over at Mossgiel. He thinks of the woe that waits on Jean, of the dismay of her family, and of the world's pointed finger. Poor bard! hardly beset by the nemesis of his own seven-times heated passions, he makes the best reparation he can. He is not base to desert her whom still he loves, nor to cast off the babe whose coming brings dishonor, but is ready with a written testimonial that she is his wedded wife, though the marriage be "secret and irregular." Whether the blessing or banning of church and society be his, he is ready to claim her as his own, and shield her from scorn and malediction.

But a sad surprise awaits him. The sturdy mason
of Mauchline, who is not highly gifted with pity or
magnanimity, peremtorily excludes him. He will
accept the shame he has entailed, if it must be, but
he will by no means accept him to be a son-in-law.
The canny, prudent man, who looks well to the
honor of his family, is roused at last. There is a
stormy scene in the house, and he is white with rage.
In his fury he denounced "the rake-helly Burns,"—
of whom he wanted nothing but the chance to lay
hands on him,—and demanded that his daughter re-
linquish him forever. Scorn, contempt and indignation made the sorrowing man their target. Why
was such a villain permitted to cumber the earth!
So was the poet pursued,—"skulking," as he de-
clares, day after day, "from covert to covert, under
the terrors of a jail," while

"Hungry ruin had him in the wind."

The righteousness of men in Scotland once sent
them to "the munitions of rocks," with the sword
of Claverhouse behind them; but now Caledon's
sweetest singer, who, like another hill-hunted minstrel, had reason to cry.—"I am a sinful man, O,
Lord," is driven in the tracks of the Cameronians,
and seeks refuge in Grampian glens from the pursū-
ing sheriff. As for Armour, he can still care for his
daughter. He bids her burn to ashes the precious
paper that might show Burns to have any legal claim
upon her. So easy-hearted Jean submits, is with-
drawn within the privacy of home, while Burns has
reason to suppose the gate so firmly barred he may
come to her no more.

Here, was it a ray of heavenly light, or flame of
earthly passion, that shot across the background of
this accumulated shadow and disorder, in the ro-

mantic episode of Highland Mary? We cannot
pause to trace the event, to delineate her features,
vaguely seen, to reconcile what is perhaps the irrecon-
cilable, so as, on the moral basis of society, to justify
her or her lover. Enough to affirm, it was an event
of which poetry could be made; and, whatever she
was in sober fact, we see her only through the misty
gold of song; for, in the haunted region where the
poet's fancy has placed her, consecrated by his
yearning, adoring, affectionate regret, she is forever
beautiful and fair, beyond earth and time and the
touch of contamination.

Mary being gone, Jean snatched from him, and
with the scourge of society at his back, the unhappy
bard meditates flight from his native country. He
craves the remembrance of his companions at Tarbolton,—

" Dear brethren of the mystic tie,"—

when he is afar. He goes over the moors at evening, singing his farewell song to Caledonia, in
musical memory,

" Pursuing past unhappy loves."

Already a tossing world of waters is in his eye, and
the doom of that " fatal, deadly shore,"—which,
please Heaven, he shall never see! Fancy Robert
Burns, the Poet of Freedom, a slave-driver at the
line! If Moore's soul was vexed by the lazy Ber-
mudian solitude, what uneasy soul will fret itself
away from Jamaica, should he ever live to reach it!
Let such a business, in such a climate, be delegated
to Mr. M'Lehose; and Burns will be better off riding over Ayrshire hills and Galway moors, " searching auld wives' barrels." His heart, at least, is at
home. We kiss again the hand of Fate—dealer of

so many untoward things—and bless the propriety
of that combination of circumstances which saved
him from so palpable an absurdity.

But how near he came to taking the step! He
went so far as to engage his passage in the steerage
of a vessel soon to leave the Clyde. But before he
can do this he must be "master of nine guineas."
And where shall he get "nine guineas?" Poetry is
sometimes a golden lode, but not always. But
Burns has friends, who advise him to collect and
publish his poems, and who will subscribe liberally;
so "Wee Johnnie" of Kilmarnock is engaged to
print six hundred precious copies, that with the prod-
uct thereof Scotland's greatest poet may be able to
go and bury himself! But that book became the
step-ladder to Fame. Coila was there at the poet's
shoulder and motioned him to ascend. Drummond,
Dunbar, Ramsay, Fergusson,—you have done your
best; but never book of yours was like this one,
done at Kilmarnock! Like fire among whin bushes
or dry heather on the moors, so spread the flame his
genius had enkindled. His was at once a song of
such repute that the lady in her castle, the minister
in his manse, the philosopher and literateur in his
study, the herdsman and ploughman on the hills,
the servant girl in the kitchen,—all, and all classes,
seized eagerly on that wonderful book, thankful to
get it at three shillings,—and to pore upon it, forgetful of all else, by the hour. What next? Of
course he shall hear from good and worthy Dr.
Blacklock! Of course farewells are taken back,
"old Coila's hills and dales" reclaim him, while
mounted on a steed furnished at his hand, and *en
route* to Edinburgh, his is a triumphal progress all
the way!

We might dwell on his astonishing career in that

city, but Jean does not figure there. She is in humiliation and obscurity. Meanwhile her lover, for a time, seems to cast a lustre on the street as he walks, and the young Jeffreys of the time are gazing after him. He sits with the magnates and drains their wine, while they beam upon the prodigy; and when he opens his lips in speech or song they behold their own Scotland, as Mirza beheld the valley of Bagdat when enchanted by the presence of the genius. Alas! when he was gone they were drinkers, and diners, and hunters, and kneader's of common clay, just the same! Then, the glamor gone, the gold dimmed,—his fine eyes and bold, bright speech no longer a novelty,—he may retreat a social step or two, and finally subside to the pothouse; since, in their view, he seems to have for that station some affinity. And what is our station in life? Is it not that whereunto we are born, or into which we are cast, sometimes with little respect to our fitness therefor? But for the pothouse, which caught the shimmer of his matchless verse, would that that open door to death had been closed to him, and that the rich and great had beguiled him away from the place where his self control was broken down. He was bowing with the weary burden of a youth that had wrenched his nerves and stooped his shoulders; and what heavy weights, alas! each successive year should lay there! We sorrow to think how his life was preyed upon and frittered away. Are our brethren of the flesh set thus to waste us? Is it true, as the wise Goethe said, that we must be either sledge or anvil? Must creation be abolished, indeed, before that part of it that preys upon the other can be done away? It is a disheartening question, if we wait for the answer.

Clarinda, the new "mistress of his soul," over

whom he languished in Edinburgh—another of his
half ideal and wholly mistaken loves—cannot detain
us.   Whatever may be said of the real depth and
sincerity of that attachment on the poet's part, (the
devotion of poor Agnes cannot be dubious,) it occasioned that singular self-revelation of the weakness
and strength of Burns, read nowhere so clearly as in
the "Sylvander" letters;—yea, and moreover, some
of the sweetest, saddest songs in any language,—
notably that one concerning which Scott declared
that four lines of it "contained the essence of a
thousand love-tales."   Burns, destined to immortality and the tomb; Agnes, with her voluptuous
beauty, to wear into wrinkled age, and to make the
tearful record of the sixth December, 1831,—"This
day I never can forget.   Parted with Robert Burns
in the year 1791, never more to meet in this world.
Oh, may we meet in heaven!"   Amen!   Love there
may be no wrong.

   Think you that must have been a proud, if not, a
glad day, when the young man—who had carried
duchesses off their feet by the stroke of his eloquent
lips, and turned their heads with his unlacquered
brilliancy—set his face away from the city, where he
had gathered and worn his ripest laurels, toward
that cottage of the west where those who loved him
still struggled with their poverty?   Not prouder will
he be to greet them all, than will be that fond,
forgiving mother—on whose knee sits the little
daughter whose coming had been with shadow—to
see her boy again, with the smiles of Edinburgh yet
reflected from his face.   God bless that mother's
memory!   Untroubled be her rest in the churchyard
at Bolton, in the vale of Tyne, who sung the music
into her poet's soul, and who should now be sleeping
by the side of William Burness, near the old kirk of

Alloway.   But Burns, with his five hundred pounds sterling from publisher Creech, may come home to Mossgiel and help to lift Gilbert's burdens, and give cheer to all about him;—for what a change to his worldly affairs and prospects the past few months have brought!

The same stroke of fortune that brought him competence and fame, put him in popular favor at home, blotted out all wrongs, and restored to him his Jean,—whom all the while he loved, and whom he now married in right good earnest!   Armour is now complacent and interposes no barrier.   And quite human and natural it was, doubtless, as Stoddard regards it, for Armour now to open his door, to give him his hand, and permit Jean to act her pleasure.   We are not unwilling to see Demos placated by some borrowed regard for the singing shepherds, and the course of true love, so coldly checked, running free and smooth again.   Wrath cannot burn forever in a stone-mason's bosom; and, after all, is not Burns, penitent, and impecunious, a scandal to the country-side, stealing kisses and making mock marriages, one sort of person; and Burns, triumphant, belauded, independent and replenished, quite another?   Certainly!   At least nine out of every ten persons will think so, when they come to the question of marrying and giving in marriage.

Now we come to that era in the life of Burns the contemplation of which has always given us the highest pleasure, and which, on the whole, we regard as the happiest, noblest, and most hopeful, the poet was ever to know.   He had written his domestic philosophy in four memorable lines,—

> "To make a happy fireside clime
> For weans and wife—
> That's the true pathos and sublime
> Of human life;—"

and we honor him for his heroic attempt to realize
this in actual experience, though the struggle ended
in partial defeat. Well for him could a modicum of
useful dullness,—the ballast of a nature like Wordsworth's—have been infused into him. The cup of
his delight must needs be foaming at the brim, or
lying insipid in the lees. He knew no middle course.
Dullness was like lead upon his spirits, and if mirth
and wit and wisdom were not at the flood, (putting
aside all other distresses,) then

> " He could lie down like a tired child,
> And weep away this life of care,"

that had him chained, at once as Fortune's pet and
victim.

Yet, with some of the joy of his new-found love,
and the light of his young fame, about him, we follow him to Ellisland, on the Nith, where Lord Dalswinton has leased him a farm, and where, if he is to
cherish a wife and bring up children, he must set
about rearing a home. We see him here, as we see
the flowers at dawn, and hear him as we hear the
birds at the sun-rising. He treads the fields he can
almost call his own, and accumulates rock and lime,
and other materials, to build his cottage. What
matters now that his own head is sheltered by a
hovel, and that no smiling cook caters to his appetite,
won from the fresh-turned mould and the caller air!
He has come home to nature again, to love and song,
—and wherefor not to content? He has come back
to the " gay green birk " and the blossoming haw-
thorn, the wildbrier rose, the fox glove, the hare
bell, and the mountain daisy, he loved so well;—
back where he can hear again "the loud solitary
whistle of the curlew in summer noon, or the wild
mixing cadence of a troop of gray plover in an

autumnal morning." We see him standing with the muse in the midst of his fair acres, and around him the Whitsuntide birds are singing, and down below the green and woody bank the clear Nith waters go rippling on with a melody like that waking in his own heart. We see him, mounted on horseback, thridding the dale, through which the river flows, to Dumfries; or speeding over the hills to Ayrshire, for a glimpse at Jean and the folks; or directing his plough along the furrowed slope; or working at his cottage, which stands at this day, in part the work of his hands; "or with a white sheet containing his seed corn, slung across his shoulders, striding with measured steps along his turned-up furrows, and scattering the grain in the earth;" or, "pursuing the defaulters of the revenue, among the hills and vales of Nithside, his roving eye wandering over the charms of nature, and muttering his wayward fancies as he moves along," His muse, long bound with the silken fetters of Edinburgh, was now liberated, to sing a clearer, blither carol,—a song one never hears but his heart leaps up, as Wordsworth declared his did, when he beheld "a rainbow in the sky."

Yes, happy he was here, if poet such as he can ever be happy. Jean has come at autumntide; their housekeeping is set up, and the children, who had been their sorrow, have already begun to comfort them. Burns teaches them the catechism, and tries to be a good father to them, as he remembers one who once was such to him. Even

" The big ha-Bible, ance his father's pride,"

is sometimes opened, and used devoutly, as in that home where he was in the place of an elder son after that sire had gone. Jenny Geddes, "the auld mare,"

will not need so often to carry him "over the Cum-
nock hills," for the lode-star that drew him to Ayrshire is in Nithsdale now. The new "biggin" being ready, they went into it. On the day when the
new abode was to be christened, Burns, who "delighted to keep up the old-world *freits* or usages,"
bade Betty Smith, the servant, "take a bowl of salt,
and place the family Bible on the top of it, and,
bearing these, walk first into the new house and
possess it," while "he himself, with his wife on his
arm, followed Betty and the Bible and the salt, and
so entered their new abode."

But, even in this retirement, and amid the soli-
tudes of his favorite country, great despairs and dis-
gusts came over him. Sometimes duchesses and
lords and the elite of Edinburgh walked in his
vision, and the mirth of gilded tables rang in his
ears. Then the humble peasantry of whom he
came,—the "hardy sons of rustic toil," the sight of
whose smoking firesides in the quiet gloaming filled
his eyes with benignant tears and his heart with
blessings, dwindled in his eyes to ignorant churls,
unfit for his association. "The only things," he
said, in some such mood, to Bengo, the engraver,
"that are to be found in this country in any degree
of perfection are stupidity and canting." What to
them was Coila's laureate in comparison with the
steady-going farmer, who attended to his fields, and
kept his accounts straight? "Prose," he declared,
"they only knew in graces and sermons, which they
valued, like plaiding webs, by the ell; while a poet
and a rhinoceros suggested ideas equally distinct
and agreeable." The fact is, his farming did not
prosper; only poetry and the excise turned out well.
It seemed that nature, who had given him the harvest of the eye and heart, had consistently denied

him any other out of her fields; for why should even a poet have everything? How hard is this rural existence to dignify and adorn! Horace and Cowley had tried and praised it; but they had never tried to dig out a living and pay rent from the wet clay of Ellisland. "Dr. Moore had mentioned the friendliness of husbandry to fancy, while he wished for him the prosperous union of the farmer and the poet. But Burns had neither Mæcenas for a landlord nor Horace for a neighbor." But he gave the tribute of a glowing admiration to such small poets as the country then furnished. It seems as if an astral lamp bowed to the tallow candles.

Dear Ellisland! First home of Robert Burns, and his wedded Jean, we love to linger with you! Here he exulted in song, as husband never exulted before:

> " By night, by day, a-field, at hame,
>   The thoughts o'thee my breast inflame;
> And aye I muse and sing thy name—
>   I only live to love thee."

You seem to feel the leap of the warm blood in that verse; you seem to hear the rollic rapture of a boblink, dancing on a spray, in the eye of his mate. The stately epithalmiums of the poets are diminished before it. Dear Ellisland! the poet's sanctuary and refuge, his best bower of song,—why came that sad necessity of leaving you? What though he rode through ten parishes his weekly two hundred miles; he was back to Jean again, and the worst that came here was better than the dull misery of Mossgiel. Was it good to give up the cozy cottage his own hands had builded, and the "hazelly glens" of the Nith, with his pleasant outlook of woods and waters, for mean Dumfries, the Wee Vennel, the dirty and sordid streets and alleys? But necessity is a stern master; and Dante's exile and Tasso's prison teach us that, for poets, as for ordinary mortals, there is appointed a destiny that we all must learn to dree.

Whatever storms came here the skies were often fair, and such starry influences rose over him as had only blessed his boyhood. For is it not true that love in its first blush kindles a new youth-tide? Here his first winter of married life "glided happily" away, while "golden days of the heart and the fancy often shone, when the father rejoiced in the crown of the poet." Down by yonder riverside Jeans aw him, bewitched, inspired,—stalking past her with shining visionary eyes, gesticulating with his arms, and rabbling off verses,—his brain hot with the throes of Tam O'Shanter!

> "Kings may be blest, but he was glorious,
> O'er a' the ills o' life victorious!"

Out in yonder stack-yard, prone on the ground, did not his wife find him in a realm of rapture, his eyes fixed upon the kindling star of dawn then shinning with lessening ray? Could she know that then was born in his soul a lyric cry to which the heart of every after age should tremble, to the end of time? Here, to this new shrine of song, came many a visitor—now and then one not altogether mean or obscure,—among them "the fat and festive Grose," who let fall his

> "Fouth o' all nick-nackets,
> Rusty airn caps and jinglin' jackets,"

to hear from the poet's own lips "of the wonderful jump of Cutty Sark and the magnificent terrors of Tam."

It is a curiously entertaining glimpse we get of Burns and his wife, as entertainers, while yet they lived in the Ellisland cottage, through the eyes of the English writer, Samuel Egerton Bridges. Drawn by the fame of the new bard, and by admiration for his genius, he came seeking an interview; but, fearing that Burns might be in a mood unfavorable to a gracious reception, proceeded cautiously, and reconnoitred the neighborhood:

"About a mile from his residence, on a bench under a tree, I passed a figure which, from the engraved portraits of him, I did not doubt was the poet, but I did not venture to address him. On arriving at his cottage, Mrs. Burns opened the door; she was the plain sort of humble woman she had been described. She ushered me into a neat apartment, and said that she would send for Burns, who had gone for a walk. In about half an hour he came, and my conjecture proved right; he was the person I had seen on the bench by the roadside. At first I was not entirely pleased with his countenance, I thought it had a sort of capricious jealousy, as if he was half inclined to treat me as an intruder. I resolved to bear it, and try if I could humor him. I, let him choose his turn of conversation, but said a word about the friend whose letter I had brought to him. It was now about four in the afternoon of an autumn day. While we were talking, Mrs. Burns, as if accustomed to entertain visitors in this way, brought in a bottle of Scotch whiskey, and set the table. I accepted this hospitality. I could not help observing the curious glance with which he watched me at the entrance of this sequel of homely entertainment. He was satisfied; he filled our glasses, "Here's a health to auld Caledonia!" The fire sparkled in his eye, and mine sympathetically met his. He shook my hands and we were friends at once. Then he drank, 'Erin forever!' and the tear

of delight burst from his eye. The fountain of his
mind and of his heart opened at once, and flowed
with abundant force almost till midnight. He had
an amazing acuteness of intellect as well as glow of
sentiment.   *   *   *   I never conversed
with a man who appeared to be more warmly impressed with the beauties of nature, and visions of
female beauty and tenderness seemed to transport
him. He did not merely appear to be a poet at casual intervals, but at every moment a poetical enthusiasm seemed to beat in his veins, and he lived all
his days the inward if not the outward life of a poet.
I thought I perceived in Burns' cheek the symptoms
of an energy which had been pushed too far, and he
had this feeling himself. Every now and then he
spoke of the grave so soon to close over him. His
dark eye had at first a character of sternness, but as
he became warm, though this did not entirely melt
away, it was mingled with changes of extreme
softness."

Praise to Jean, also,—as steadfast in courage and
gentleness and duteous affection, as her husband was
in intellect and genius. We have little heart to follow her to Dumfries, the scene of her deepest
sorrows and of her heaviest cares. She disappears
within the walls of home, and we get few glimpses
of her; but we cannot doubt that hers were ever-in-
creasing privations and anxieties. Her husband is
oftener and longer from home, more exposed to peril
and mischance, more reckless and abandoned, at the
last, and more in questionable company. Yes, she
bears her part, though we see little of her; still she
keeps "her fireside clime" by dint of as brave a
heart as then beat in the breast of a woman, and
made an asylum for her wayward Robin, when stung
with the whips and arrows "of outrageous fortune."

He is still before us,—a figure, now noble, now pathetic, but always appealing, commanding, our sympathies. We see him riding, with Mr. Syme, over Galway moors in the rain, drenched and chill without, but his bosom in a "bleeze" with the martial fires of Caledonia, and the splendid conception of "Scots wha hae wi' Wallace bled." We see him as he lifts his glass to toast the nobler name than that of Pitt,—a spirited act that brought him under the eye and hand of official jealousy. We see him sheering away from the gala-day crowd who dared to scorn him on the streets of Dumfries,—cut to the heart that once was so light, but has been so broken. We see him at the well of Brow, on the Solway shore,—the signet of death already on his brow. We see him sitting at the table of Mrs. Craig, widow of the minister of Ruthwell, and the setting sun shines full upon his face. His words, accompanied with a smile of the sweetest benignity, spoken to the daughter of his hostess, when, observant, she stepped to drop the curtain,—are among the saddest, the most pathetic, he ever uttered: "Thank you, my dear, for your kind attention: but oh! let him shine: he will not shine long for me." In all these scenes, and in many others, we see him moving, and his acts, like his words, are given to fame; but Jean, who loved him, as they can who love with prayers and deeds, is seen of few, and seen not at all heroically, except in that light wherein He sees who sees truly the heroes and martyrs of the fireside,—many of whose names are soon forgotten on the earth, though they are written in Heaven.

She was a true wife; she could more than forgive. To her, after her husband had gone, his memory was radiant, and the very color of his faults faded away. The largeness of her heart had something of divineness in it; and it was no small tribute to her erring lover when she could say of him, years after his death, while conversing with the Ettrick Shepherd: "He never said a misbehadden word to me a' the days o' his life." Then, I will venture to say, were he here to declare himself, he could utter as much of her. Mild of speech, gentle of heart, prudent and discreet, she could soothe and charm his perturbed spirit, and settle his cares to rest. Was any other woman he ever loved and sung so fitted to him? Highland Mary might beckon him from Heaven, but Jean Armour steadied his sometime faltering step upon the earth.

She survived him till the lichens had time to grow upon his gravestone; till his dust had been exhumed and grandly ensepulchred again. She lived to a serene and beautiful age; she saw the star of his fame ascended high, and knew him, by universal rumor, one of the greatest poets of all time. She lived, honored, respected, beloved, and dwelt among her children and her children's children. In her widowhood she abode, and held the name and memory of her consort sacred, nor ever pined for another manly arm to lean upon. Before Hew Ainslie left Scotland for America, he called upon her;—and, while he opens the door, we get a peep at her in her closing years:

"It was," as Thomas Latto relates, "in a somewhat pensive mood that he sought and entered Mrs. Burns' humble cottage, where she lived in comparative comfort and unquestioned respectability, supported to a great extent by the bounty of Lord Panmure; who, though he refused to contribute more than a paltry pittance for the maintenance of his son and heir, the Hon. Fox Maule, was pleased to indulge one of his crotchets by donating £100 per annum to Robert Burns' struggling, half-destitute widow. She was overrun with visitors, but the stranger introducing himself, she received him in her kindly motherly way. His manner was very winning when not oppressed by a sense of conde-cending patronage, and of that Jean had none. They got unco pack an' thick thegither in less time than it takes to tell it, and of course the dead poet formed the staple of 'the twa-handed crack.' She commun-icated to him a good deal that has now passed from a usually retentive memory. 'Fowr oors' was just approaching, and the venerable dame proceeding to 'mask' her tea, courteously invited him to remain and share the refreshing cup. They talked of relic hunters, and she professed herself utterly aweary of them and their pertinacity. She spoke almost cheerily of the 'roup' of their furniture after the great man's death, and of the 'awful' prices realized by eight-day clock, dilapidated 'chairs, pans, grid-dles, etc.' 'But oh!' she said jokingly, 'if they were to be sell't noo they wad bring twenty times mair.' Hew wanted to take a short walk in some of the bard's haunts, and she immediately looked for a shawl to accompany him. 'I'm thinkin,' remarked our young man, 'that can hardly be the shawl ye got frae George Thomson.' 'No quite,' was her simple reply, 'that wad need to hae been well hained to last so long. It's sax an' thretty years sin' he made me that present.' They walked together to Lincluden Abbey, I think—at any rate to a ruin—and she stood for a moment on a certain sheltered and lovely spot. 'It was just here,' she observed, 'that my man aften paused, and I believe made up mony a poem an' sang ere he cam' in to write it doun. He was never fractious—aye gude natured and kind baith to the bairns and to me.' Hew felt then, as he did long afterwards, that Jean, of all the women in the world, was the one specially fitted to be the poet's life-long companion. Clarinda had a dangerous 'spunk' about her, and would have stood no nonsense nor tolerated his admitted aberrations. Mary Campbell, though gentle and amiable, had yet Highland blood in her veins, and the ire of the scions of Macallum is sometimes easily roused and not so easily laid. But Jean was indulgent, patient, affectionate, gentle, good, and above all, forgiving. She was by no means the untidy woman she has been represented. Her skin and complexion, even in advanced age, were fine, and she might be considered a comely, as she was unquestionably a pleasant, woman. When they returned from the trip, Ainslie proposed taking his immediate departure, but before leaving, grasping her hand, he said: 'I wad like weel ere I gae, if ye wad permit me to kiss the cheek o' Burns' faithfu' Jean, to be a reminder to me o' this meetin' when I'm far awa.' She laughed, held up her face to him and said: 'Aye, lad, an' welcome.' So he printed a kiss on her still unwithered lips, and that was the last he saw of Jeanie Armour."

Her memory is still fragrant, and, with that of her husband,—whom she survived for a term of years equal to the whole duration of his earthly life, —forms a part of that haunted landscape. She is held dear, for his sake and for her own. Just now beneath our eyes lies a rude engraving of Bonnie Jean, and of her little granddaughter,—a slip of a girl, who stands beside the seated matron, enfolding her neck with a slender arm. A white frilled headdress gives an appearance of unusual fullness, almost of puffiness, to the face,—a face that is still fair, if not beautiful. These are the same winning eyes that captivated Burns, the same motherly linea-

ments that Ainslie looked upon and that Latto described. Dark curling locks partially escape from
her cap's border, and the lips and nose suggest none
of the shrinking or pinching that comes with age.
It is an engaging and lovable face, with the bright-
ness and freshness that belong to flowers and running water,—so that I marvel not her poet sang of
her:

> "I see her in the dewy flowers,
>   I see her sweet and fair;
> I hear her in the tunfu' birds,
>   I hear her charm the air:
> There's not a bonnie flower that springs
>   By fountain, shaw, or green;
> There's not a bonnie bird that sings
>   But minds me o' my Jean."

THE BEST WIFE FOR BURNS.

By George Gebbie.

Jean Armour was the best wife Burns could have married, when we consider his education and early associations, and all the circumstances surrounding him. She was good-looking, healthy, industrious, thrifty. She was, moreover, what Burns wanted most in a wife, forgiving, and he must have a strange mind who says that she didn't love him with a devotion undivided and unwavering. Had Burns been born, reared and educated otherwise than he was, it might have been allowable to suppose that a better wife than Jean Armour could have been selected for him; but as circumstances found him, we say, she was the best wife for him. Had he married "Clarinda" or Margaret Chalmers, both of whom could have appreciated him as a poet, there would have been some congenial days and weeks, perhaps, but in the long run we do not believe that they could have controlled the wayward "Son of Song" any more than Jean did, especially when we remember the Scotland of the days of Burns. True, a woman of strong character would have tried to correct him and keep him straight, and there is just where the trouble would have come in. Burns would have kicked over the traces, the harness would have been broken, and mending it would only have more rapidly hastened the catastrophe which was fated to occur. Jean had advantages of position which Burns had not,—the association of local acquaintance between herself and her husband, and all the glamour of an early and fervent love between the two. Then, their children existed, and her appreciation of him (we have his own statement for it) was unbounded; and we also know from his own letters that in music, she was a kindred spirit, as his frequent references to her "Woodnotes wild," bear ample witness.

BURNS'S BONNIE JEAN.

By Angus Ross, Glasgow,

Author of "Home and other Poems."

Great Dukes and Earls may find a place,
　On History's hoary page;
And ladies fair of stately grace,
　May poet's pen engage,
Be mine to sing the praises due
　To Burns's Bonnie Jean.

By fate's decree of lowly birth,
　And in a cottage bred;
Yet was her heart of truest worth,
　Her soul with truth inlaid,
And fair like gowan on the green
　Was Burns's Bonnie Jean.

Tho' oft the bard in lofty strains
　Did of his country sing;
Of Bruce and Wallace and their trains
　He made the echoes ring;
But aye he poured his sweetest strains
　In praise of Bonnie Jean.

While Bonnie Doon flows to the sea,
　And flowers spring to be pressed,
While little birds sing merrily,
　And love stirs human breast,
Of noble women she'll be queen,
　This Burns's Bonnie Jean.

THE HOME LIFE OF BURNS AND JEAN ARMOUR.

Dumfries Letter to the London Times, Dec. 7, 1887.

The south-western region of Scotland—Dumfries and Galloway—lying toward the sun on the northern shore of the Solway, is not much sought after by lovers of picturesque scenery. It lies out of the beaten track of tourists and wonder hunters. In comparison with the solemn grandeur of the Highland mountains and glens and the stern ruggedness of the west coast, it is nowhere. Rich beauty rather than sterile sublimity is its most prominent characteristic history, antiquity and modern literature add the charms of association to the scenery in a way that is quite unique. The ruins of Cærlaverock and Lochmaben and Thrieve Castles remind us of feudal times. The ruins of Dundrennan, Sweetheart, and Lincluden Abbeys carry us back to the monastic age. Carsluith and Ravenshall tell us that we are in the land of Scott—of Guy Mannering and Redgauntlet. Ellisland and Dumfries conjure us into the land of Burns, associated as they are with the scenes of "Scots wha hae" and "Auld Lang Syne," and "Duncan Gray," and many other of the choicest lyrics of the ploughman bard. Unquestionably it is their later literary associations that constitute the potent spell that attracts wanderers, enthusiastic, though comparatively few, to this region of Scotland. If any proof of this were required, it would be found in the fact that the great majority of the pilgrims whose curiosity leads them into the district are neither Englishmen nor Scotsmen, but are Americans. Americans care very little for feudal times—for Maxwel's or Johnstons, or Kirkpatricks, for monks or for nuns—but they care a great deal for Meg Merrilles and Bertram of Ellangowan, for Robert Burns and Bonnie Jean, for Highland Mary and Tam o'Shanter. And here Burns rather than Scott, is the potent attraction. All Scotland is the land of Scott—from Sumburg Head to Kirkmaiden; but there are, as every one knows, two Lands of Burns. There is the Ayrshire land, in which the poet spent his youth and his early manhood; and there is the Dumfriesshire land, in which he spent the last eight years of his life, which proved at once his saddest and his most brilliant as well as his most prolific days. It is of Dumfriesshire as the scene of the greatest trials and the greatest triumphs of the life of Burns, as his last home on earth and the cherished resting-place of his ashes, that I wish to speak in this letter.

Burns was in his thirtieth year when he made a fresh start in life as tenant of the farm of Ellisland, about five miles north of the town of Dumfries. He was newly married to Jean Armour; he had visited Edinburgh, and his reputation as a poet was fairly established. He was full of the energy of early manhood, and fortune seemed to be smiling on his efforts to establish for himself a permanent home. The present farm-house of Ellisland, on the right bank of the gently flowing Nith, was built for Burns after he entered on the tenancy of the farm. It is a long, low, not uncomfortable one-story house of four rooms, and it is now in much the same state in which it was then, excepting that the room which Burns used as a kitchen is now a bedroom. Burns's parlor is still the parlor of the house. Lines scratched with a diamond on the windows of this and

another room profess to be from the poet's hand, as
he had a well-known fondness for making his mark
in that way; but these Ellisland lines are of more
than doubtful authenticity.   It is interesting to think
that these rooms constituted the home of Burns during the happiest, or at least the most hopeful days of
his life.   It is more interesting perhaps to go outside
and to feel that these are the very woods and fields
and river on which the poet's eye rested, and whence
he drew some of his natural inspiration.   Across the
Nith are the woods of Dalswinton, and what was
then the residence of Burns's ingenious and sympathetic landlord, Miller, the inventor of the steam-
boat.   About a mile higher up the Nith on his own
side are the pleasant bowers of Friar's Carse, where
lived his good friend Capt. Riddel of Glenriddel;
and between them was the Hermitage, then a charm·
ing rustic retreat, to which Riddel gave the poet a
private key.   Close at hand is the Nith itself, which
was to Burns a perpetual joy—" Winding Nith,"
"Wandering Nith," "Sweet Nith"—sharer of his
secrets and sole witness of many of his poetical
paroxysms.   Many were the pleasant walks he had
by the green bank of the river between Ellisland
and Friar's Carse, but to him doubtless the path was
also strewn with sad and serious memories, such as
those which led him on one occasion to pause at the
Hermitage and moralize in the character of "The
Beadsman of Nith-side."   It would be interesting to
have some record of his thoughts as he traversed
this path to and from the famous drinking tourna-
ment at Friar's Carse, which he attended as umpire
and chronicler, and which he immortalized in the
poem beginning:

"I sing of a whistle, a whistle of worth."

A few nights later, in the barnyard at Ellisland, a
fit of deepest melancholy gave place to a divine
ecstacy, out of which came the sublime verses, "To
Mary in Heaven." Burns made and sometimes
wrote his finest poems in the open air. There is a
haugh by the river below Ellisland which was the
scene of some of his grandest "poetic pains." Once
he agonized there for a whole day, pacing the green-
sward from end to end, now muttering or crooning
to himself, now pausing by the dike-side to put down
a thought or a verse, and before the sun had set he
had completed "Tam o'Shanter"—"since Bruce
fought Bannockburn," says Alexander Smith, "the
best single day's work done in Scotland." Here,
also, before his wife had joined him, he had given
voice to his lonely yearnings in that tenderest of low
lyrics, "Of a' the airts the wind can blaw." At
Ellisland, too, Burns wrote his incomparable farewell to "Clarinda"

> "Ae fond kiss and then we sever."

of one stanza which—the fourth—Scott said that it
contained "the essence of a thousand love tales."
These are the now famous lines:

> "Had we never loved sae kindly,
> Had we never loved sae blindly,
> Never met or never parted—
> We had ne'er been broken-hearted."

But at Ellisland the poet's muse was much more
prolific than his farm. Though for a year he had
conjoined with his farm the post of gauger or excise
officer, with a salary of £50 a year, he found himself, at the end of 1791 in such straitened circumstances that he was forced to throw up his lease and
to remove to the town of Dumfries, trusting to his

office in the excise for his only means of livelihood.
In Dumfries, Burns, with his wife and three sons,
took up his abode in a house of three rooms on the
second floor of a tenement in the "Wee Vennel,"
now Bank street. About two years afterward he removed to a better house, self-contained, in Mill
street, or the Mill-hole Brae, but now called Burns
street, and there he spent the remainder of his days.
Both of these houses are now objects of interest to
pilgrims to the poet's shrine, especially the latter, in
which one sees the little parlor in which Burns enjoyed the sweets of home life, and the bedroom in
which he died. It is satisfactory to know that the
house in Burns street, which Mrs. Burns (Jean
Armour) occupied till her death, in 1834, was purchased by the poet's family and committed to the
custody of Public Trustees, who are bound to uphold
it forever. It is occupied by the master of the in-
dustrial school built on the adjoining land, which
bears on its front a tablet recording the fact of
Burns residence there, and surmounted by a bust of
the poet. Dumfries was then, as it is still, one of
the handsomest of the provincial capitals of Scotland.
"Queen of the South" it proudly calls itself, and
there is not a little of regal splendor in its spires and
towers, and in its commanding site on the banks of
the Nith. There are points in the town from which
magnificent views are obtained of Nithsdale, with
Lincluden Abbey in the middle distance, and Queens-
berry Hill crowning the surrounding heights. Then,
even more than now, Dumfries was a noted fashionable resort, in which Edinburgh being too far. dis-
tant and London being out of the question, the local
nobility and gentry had their town residences. By
the intellectual society Burns was well received, at
least until his political opinions, still more than his

social eccentricities—for the latter were those of the time and ought to have gained him sympathy rather than aversion—brought him into collision with the apostles of good society. Though the persecutors of Burns have gone to their own place, Dumfries still rings with the name of Burns from end to end. A marble statue of Burns, recently erected, fills the place of honor in the streets of the town. The Mausoleum of Burns, in St. Michael's Churchyard, is the entire attraction to all from far or near who visit the place. The site of his pew in St. Michael's Church—for the pew itself was long ago purchased and carried off by a devoted admirer—is regarded with subdued reverence. The parlor in the Globe Tavern—"Burns's Howff"—in which he spent many a merry evening, and in which his favorite chair, occupying the Poet's Corner, is still sacredly preserved, is a point of interest which no pilgrim would dream of omitting.

Unhappily, the same Globe Tavern has been the cause of endless misconceptions of the poet's good name. It has been assumed that, because he was a frequenter of taverns, he was therefore a hopelessly abandoned character and an unmitigated sot. Those who leap to this conclusion are forgetful of the times and of the custom of the times in which Burns lived. They forget that the tavern was in those days what the daily newspaper is in these—the only available means of acquiring and of discussing the news of the day. That Burns, in his pursuit of social intercourse, sometimes drank to excess cannot be denied; but that he was a habitual drunkard is the reverse of the truth. The best proof of this is found in the fact, which is on record on the testimony of his wife, and of those who knew him best, that Burns was never known to drink to excess in his own house. His faults, grave as they were, were those of his time, and not of the man. No one, therefore, who goes to Dumfries and who drinks to the immortal memory of the bard in the Globe Tavern need be troubled with "compunctious visitings" on the ground that he is commemorating the fatal orgies of a confirmed bacchanalian. Burns was nothing of that kind. He had his weaknesses and his faults, like other men—more than other men, because of his tenderly strung and super-sensitive nature, of a pulse that "ran like a ratton"—and mightily he suffered for them. But the sentimental prudery of the present day that affects abhorrence of the name of Burns because certain lordlings gave him a cold shoulder in the streets of Dumfries ought to be reminded that it was for his political far more than for his social excesses that he was made a martyr in his later days.

Infinitely more pleasant, however, than the memory of Burns as a frequenter of the Globe Tavern is it to think of him as pacing, evening after evening in Summer time, the Dock Meadow, or the banks of "winding Nith," opposite Lincluden, and excogitating the century of immortal lyrics which have endeared his name to his countrymen. Next to the Ellisland period the Dumfries period was the richest and most prolific in the history of his teeming fancy. "Duncan Gray," "Last May a braw wooer," "My heart is sair," "Ye banks and braes o' bonnie Doon," "Oh, wert thou in the cauld blast," "Scots wha hae,' and the immortal "Auld Lang Syne," are among the productions of the poet's muse in the Dumfries period. The enumeration does not suggest either mental decadence or moral deterioration. The real sadness lies in the reflection that the maker of these masterpieces of our literature, and of all literature, was at the time of their production a supervisor of excise with a salary of £70 a year, living in a house in Dumfries for which he paid no more than £8 a year rent. It is pleasant, at the same time to know that Burns has still representatives in the flesh who cherish his memory. His third son, Lieut. Col. James Glencairn Burns, left a daughter by his first marriage named Sarah, who married Dr. Berkeley Hutchison, of Cheltenham, and who has a son and three daughters. These are the great-grandchildren of the poet, and are his only direct and lawful descendants. James Burns was twice married, and by his second marriage he also left a daughter, who is still Miss Burns, and who resides at Cheltenham with her half-sister.

THE POET'S IMMORTAL WREATH FOR BONNIE JEAN.

A MAUCHLINE LADY.

When first I came to Stewart Kyle,
  My mind it was na steady,
Where'er I gaed, where'er I rade,
  A mistress still I had aye:
But when I came roun' by Mauchline town,
  Not dreadin' onie body,
My heart was caught before I thought,
  And by a Mauchline lady.

THE BELLES OF MAUCHLINE.

In Mauchline there dwells six proper young belles,
  The pride of the place and its neighborhood a',
Their carriage and dress, a stranger would guess,
  In London or Paris they'd gotten it a':

Miss Miller is fine, Miss Markland's divine,
  Miss Smith she has wit, and Miss Betty is braw:
There's beauty and fortune to get wi' Miss Morton,
  But Armour's the jewel for me o' them a'.

OH! WERE I ON PARNASSUS' HILL.

Oh, were I on Parnassus' hill!
Or had of Helicon my fill;
That I might catch poetic skill,
    To sing how dear I love thee.
But Nith maun be my muse's well,
My muse maun be thy bonnie sel';
On Corsincon I'll glow'r an' spell,
    An' write how dear I love thee.

Then come, sweet muse, inspire my lay!
For a' the lee-lang simmer's day
I couldna sing, I couldna say,
    How much, how dear I love thee.
I see thee dancing o'er the green,
Thy waist sae jimp, thy limbs sae clean,
Thy tempting lips, thy roguish een—
    By heaven an' earth I love thee.

By night, by day, a-field, at hame,
The thoughts o' thee my breast inflame;
An' aye I muse an' sing thy name—
    I only live to love thee.
Tho' I were doom'd to wander on,
Beyond the sea, beyond the sun,
Till my last weary sand was run;
    Till then—and then I love thee.

MY JEAN.

Tho' cruel fate should bid us part,
  As far's the pole and line;
Her dear idea round my heart
  Should tenderly entwine.

Tho' mountains frown and deserts howl,
  And oceans roar between;
Yet, dearer than my deathless soul,
  I still would love my Jean.

OF A' THE AIRTS THE WIND CAN BLAW.

Of a' the airts the wind can blaw,
  I dearly like the west,
For there the bonnie lassie lives,
  The lassie I lo'e best:
There wild woods grow, and rivers row,
  And mony a hill between;
But day and night my fancy's flight
  Is ever wi' my Jean.

I see her in the dewy flowers,
  I see her sweet and fair:
I hear her in the tunefu' birds,
  I hear her charm the air:
There's not a bonnie flower that springs
  By fountain, shaw, or green,
There's not a bonnie bird that sings,
  But minds me o' my Jean.

IT IS NA, JEAN, THY BONNIE FACE.

It is na, Jean, thy bonnie face,
    Nor shape that I admire,
Although thy beauty and thy grace
    Might weel awake desire.
Something in ilka part o' thee,
    To praise, to love, I find:
But dear as is thy form to me,
    Still dearer is thy mind.

Nae mair ungen'rous wish I hae,
    Nor stronger in my breast,
Than if I canna mak thee sae,
    At least to see thee blest.
Content am I, if Heaven shall give
    But happiness to thee:
And as wi' thee I'd wish to live,
    For thee I'd bear to die.

I HA'E A WIFE O' MY AIN.

I ha'e a wife o' my ain—
   I'll partake wi' naebody;
I'll tak' cuckold frae nane,
   I'll gi'e cuckold to naebody.
I ha'e a penny to spend,
   There—thanks to naebody;
I ha'e naething to lend,
   I'll borrow frae naebody.

I am naebody's lord—
   I'll be slave to naebody;
I ha'e a gude braid sword,
   I'll tak' dunts frae naebody.
I'll be merry an' free,
   I'll be sad for naebody;
If naebody care for me,
   I'll care for naebody.

THE WINSOME WEE THING.

She is a winsome wee thing,
She is a handsome wee thing,
She is a bonnie wee thing,
This sweet wee wife o' mine.

I never saw a fairer,
I never lo'ed a dearer;
And neist my heart I'll wear her,
For fear my jewel tine.

Oh leeze me on my wee thing;
My bonnie, blythesome wee thing;
Sae lang's I hae my wee thing,
I'll think my lot divine.

Tho' warld's care we share o't,
And may see meikle mair o't;
Wi' her I'll blythely bear it,
And ne'er a word repine.

THIS IS NO MY AIN LASSIE.

CHORUS.

Oh this is no my ain lassie,
    Fair tho' the lassie be;
Oh weel ken I my ain lassie,
    Kind love is in her e'e.

I see a form, I see a face
Ye weel may wi' the fairest place;
It wants to me the witching grace,
    The kind love that's in her e'e.

She's bonnie, blooming, straight, and tall,
And lang has had my heart in thrall;
And aye it charms my very saul,
    The kind love that's in her e'e.

A thief sae paukie is my Jean,
To steal a blink, by a' unseen;
But gleg as light are lovers' een,
    When kind love is in her e'e.

It may escape the courtly sparks,
It may escape the learned clerks;
But weel the watching lover marks
    The kind love that's in her e'e.

THEIR GROVES OF SWEET MYRTLE.

Their groves o' sweet myrtle let foreign lands reckon,
   Where bright-beaming summers exalt the perfume;
Far dearer to me yon lone glen o' green breckan,
   Wi' the burn stealing under the long yellow broom.

Far dearer to me are yon humble broom bowers,
   Where the blue-bell an' gowan lurk lowly unseen;
For there, lightly tripping amang the wild flowers,
   A·listening the linnet aft wanders my Jean.

Tho' rich is the breeze in their gay sunny valleys,
   An' cauld Caledonia's blast on the wave;
Their sweet sented woodlands that skirt the proud
     palace,
   What are they?—the haunt of the tyrant and
    slave!

The slave's spicy forests, and gold bubbling fountains,
   The brave Caledonian views wi' disdain;
He wanders as free as the winds of his mountains,
   Save loves willing fetters—the chains o' his Jean!

I'LL AYE CA' IN BY YON TOWN.

I'll aye ca' in by yon town,
  And by yon garden green, again;
I'll aye ca' in by yon town,
  And see my bonnie Jean, again.
There's nane sall ken, there's nane sall guess,
  What brings me back the gate again,
But she, my fairest, faithfu' lass,
  And stowlins we sall meet again.

She'll wander by the aiken tree,
  When trystin-time draws near again;
And when her lovely form I see,
  Oh, haith, she's doubly dear again!
I'll aye ca' in by yon town,
  And by yon garden green again;
I'll aye ca' in by yon town,
  And see my bonnie Jean, again.

BY WAY OF EPILOGUE.

By Hon. Charles H. Collins.

There are so many women connected with Burns that for many years the one who above all others was the source of his greatest inspiration was not at once recognized. This is the woman to whom Burns on his death bed in 1796, amid the horrors of poverty and distress made the memorable declaration " They will ken me better, Jean, a hundred years hence."

He saw then dimly as in a vision, his future fame and that his devoted wife "Bonnie Jean" would arise in glory by his side forever linked with him. Jean knew the real Burns—not the artificial. She knew that she was his fate—that she was for him, and better for him than any of those who simply represented episodes in his fitful career. Of Jean Armour none can speak but in praise. Her place is fixed in the good opinion of generations gone before and of those yet to come.

The wisest and most discriminating of Scottish writers have written of her in characters of purest ray serene and posterity has enthroned her memory as the loving, faithful, true and much enduring wife of an erratic and hard-to-manage man, who 'mid all his wanderings paid to her the truest homage of a love boundless as it was sincere. Ellison Begbie, Burns thought (at one time) would have made him happy. She did not think so, and "the Lass of Cessnock Banks" judged wisely. " My Handsome Nell " was a delightful memory, but this sweet innocent being would have made a poor life partner for the matured Burns. It required the strong will, the perfect womanhood of Jean Armour to control that proud and passion ladened soul. She tamed his remorseful notes—quelled the haunting spirits which like the Furies pursued this Modern Orestes of Scottish song judging by many of his lyrics.

To Jean the real Burns always appeared, not the fever heated brain driven by consuming flame onward to an uncertain fate. Without her his fame would have been as fitful as the luring glare of the "Will o' the wisp" over the Scottish fens. The ghouls who have ransacked every detail of the Poet's life stand silenced and abashed now at the end of the hundred years before the character of Jean who knew him better than all the world beside and forgave him all out of her great love and great true heart. The world at the end of the hundred years has without hesitation, guided by the instinct of justice, set aside even Highland Mary the immortalized deity of song and placed far above her "Bonnie Jean."

There is a little song of Burns's entitled "The Mauchline Lady" which I have always thought gave an unconscious glimpse of his own unsteadiness and of the power of Jean Armour over him from the beginning—

> "When first I came to Stewart Kyle
>   My mind it was na' steady,
> Where'er I gaed, where'er I rade,
>   A mistress still I had aye;
> But when I cam' roun' by Mauchline town,
>   Not dreadin' ony body,
> My heart was caught before I thought
>   And by a Mauchline lady."

Again in his description of the Belles of Mauchline, "Miss Miller is fine, Miss Markland's divine, Miss

Smith she has wit, and Miss Betty is braw; There's beauty and fortune to get wi' Miss Morton. But Armour's the jewel for me o' them a'."

Poor Burns, he could no more escape his destiny than the moth allured by the candle's flame, but in case of Burns it was a happy destiny and not a phantom alluring to death.

If Providence (as many suppose) fixes our ends, then the creation of Jean Armour was a necessary solvent to make Burns life complete. When the Poet contemplated his West India trip and an eternal separation from his native land, his sweetest words were for " My Jean " and not for Highland Mary. Compare and see which is from the heart:

> " Though cruel fate should bid us part,
> Far as the pole and line,
> Her dear idea round my heart
> Should tenderly entwine.
>
> Though mountains rise, and deserts howl,
> And oceans roar between :
> Yet dearer than my deathless soul,
> I still would love my Jean."

The tribute paid to Mrs. Burns in the song "Oh, were I on Parnassus Hill " speaks volumes. It was produced before she took up her residence at Ellisland as his wife. He composed it one day while gazing towards the hill of Corsincon at the head of Nithsdale and beyond which was the quiet vale where lived his " bonnie Jean."

" Of a' the airts the wind can blaw" Burns has told us he composed out of compliment to Mrs. Burns during their honeymoon. It is by many competent critics considered his best. Read that beautiful song and see the true Burns. Read it and see who was the real heroine and guiding star under

whose serene rays the fame of Burns grew. As to
how happy she made him, look at the sprightly
lines "I hae a wife o' my ain," written shortly
after the poet had welcomed home his wife to his
new house at Ellisland—the first winter he spent in
which he has described as the happiest of his life.
Burns has himself in another lyric given us a character of his wife which cannot be improved upon.
Nothing can be added to it.

> "It is na, Jean, thy bonie face,
> 　　Nor shape that I admire,
> Although thy beauty and thy grace
> 　　Might weel awake desire.
> Something, in ilk a part of thee,
> 　　To praise, to love, I find ;
> But, dear as is thy form to me,
> 　　Still dearer is thy mind.
>
> Nae mair ungenrous wish I hae,
> 　　Nor stronger in my breast,
> Than if I canna mak' thee sae,
> 　　At least to see thee blest.
> Content am I, if Heaven shall give,
> 　　But happiness to thee ;
> And as wi thee I'd wish to live,
> 　　For thee I'd bear to die."

In chapter six of "All about Burns," a former com-
plation of our present editor, I find an admirable de-
lineation of "Bonnie Jean" by Dr. Peter Ross, admirable for its fairness, its just and discriminating study
of the questions involved and creditable to the
author who places the devotion of this true woman,
wife and mother far above all future criticisim.

It is a tribute worthy of this noble woman and
worthy of the author who has seen through all the
glamour of the Mary, and Clarinda episodes and in-
stalls Bonnie Jean forever as the mistress of the
Poet's home—the true mistress of his heart.

Dr. Ross says there was one difference which speaks volumes for Jean's supremacy in the Poet's heart. "While he sang for her, she was before him with all the faults frailties and short comings of humanity; all the tedium, as it has been called of ordinary daily life while Highland Mary had passed through the veil and so become idealized long before the "lingering star" aroused in him such a force of agonized thought, and in time impelled the world, as a result of his burning words to elevate the Highland lass into one of the heroines of poetry." Jean stood her ground, conquered even Highland Mary and around her Burns has woven a garment as enduring as his own fame. In Bonnie Jean the tragic element plays no part. Pathos there is; endurance of a hard lot—a brave struggle under adverse conditions; in short, the annals of history show no truer woman, better wife or more affectionate mother than Jean Armour to whom Burns was indebted for the few happy hours he spent at home. Of all these things he is the witness. She purified him, she elevated him and guarded his fame with jealous care during the long years she survived him. May her name and memory be ever cherished by all true and faithful women who have walked up the flinty crags of time with bleeding hearts and who have stood firm to duty and untarnished by even a breath of scandal during all their days of wifehood until the end came.

To be the wife of a genius such as Burns was to be endowed with qualities such as few possess. The fate of Byron, Durer, Milton and the long drawn catalogue of unhappy unions shows this. Jean Armour proved equal to the task. Jean Armour succeeded where others would have failed. She did not quarrel; she did not upbraid; she was blind to

his follies. She was a woman of tact. She understood him thoroughly. She was his good genius.

Did you ever compare the women of Shakespeare
with those of Burns?

In the long line of shadowy figures projected on
the canvas of time by Shakespeare his women have
always appealed to the artistic sense in all lands.
Centuries have passed away, yet the endless com-
mentaries do not cease. Every one who studies
Shakespeare assumes he has found some new reason
for the characters—some occult meaning not hereto-
fore discovered. Shakespeare has furnished a battle
ground for the critics and a cause for a war of words
as to whether or not he himself was not a figure-
head; only a mere name under which the wits and
scholars of his age ventilated their political ideas.
Leaving all these controversies to those who delight
in such matters, no one can find elsewhere more perfect types of womanhood than in Shakespeare.
Imogen and Cordelia above all others are such
pictures of rare beauty of soul that it were vain to
try to imitate. The German mind would come
nearer to such ideals, but no Englishman before or
since has approached them, as indeed none of the
women of contemporary dramatists had any simil-
arity to those of Shakespeare. Trace the whole
course of literature through the 16th, 17th and 18th
centuries and until we reach Robert Burns all is
barren of the beautiful images clothed in feminine
forms which all men instinctively rise up and wor-
ship. The emotions as abstract things are often
traced. The women of Dryden, of Pope, even of
Byron have a certain lack of reality. There is no
heart in them. Gulnare, Medora, Haidee, Parasina,
in fact all of Byron's figures are Byrons in disguise.
A great poet, a great word painter yet withal a

scorner of the humble every day love which to all mankind and in all ages has seemed to be the nearest to Heaven on earth. With the coming of Robert Burns in the latter part of the 18th century there again appeared the woman who immediately took rank with the high bred heroines of Shakespeare. They were humble Scotch lassies but glorified by the pen of inspired genius and brought home to the hearts of all.

They are intensely human. Their forms, their winsome smiles glow with life on historic pages. Their beauty still beguiles the senses and Rosalind in the forest of Ardennes is not more charming than "The Lass of Ballochmyle," or "Fairest Maid on Devon Banks." The women of Shakespeare are but shadows of long ago—beautiful visions truly, but their loves and sorrows like those of Hecuba seem but as phantoms of the night, while the lassies sung by Burns stand sculptured in the light of one hundred years as plainly as seen by him. This is not art but truth. The truth which portrays our own hearts—our own women, the women of all times and ages. We love Imogen the fair daughter of Cymbeline; Cordelia the loving, brave and true; the golden haired Juliet so exquisitely wooed and won by fiery Romeo; Viola pure as the dews fresh fallen from heaven; trusting and much wronged Desdemona, yet these are not of our own time—not of our environment. These lovely creations of the dramatist's brain, restless in their loves and with lives pierced by thorns mid the flowers, with all their pleasures mingled with pain are human indeed in their way, because Shakespeare had much of Burns in his makeup as Burns had much of Shakespeare. I mean by this that each had the faculty of knowing how to put things. Each was in touch with mankind.

Every one sees something of himself, in Burns especially. Critical investigation has failed utterly to show *why* Shakespeare is so superior to all his contemporaries. *Why* he stands uniquely alone among all other writers of England, and unapproachable. So cavil, investigation and the calcium light of merciless dissection has failed to fathom the genius of Burns.

He is at the head and so easily that criticism stands rebuked. Little is known of Shakespeare. His personality is hidden in as much obscurity as that of Junius Burns is known through and through. He is part of all his creations and his heroines and himself go down the corridors of time to immortality hand in hand, the central figure being "Bonnie Jean," the queen by divine right and crowned by posterity with the wreath of Amarinthine unfading renown due to her above all others. If in song or story there is one fit to stand by her under similiar environments the pages at my command have not disclosed her. She at least seems to have had in good measure the qualities ascribed by Wordsworth. "The reason firm, the temperate will, endurance, foresight, strength and skill. A perfect woman nobly planned, to warn, to comfort and command."

BOOKS PUBLISHED

AND FOR SALE BY

THE

RAEBURN BOOK CO.,

185 GRAND STREET,

BOROUGH OF MANHATTAN,

GREATER NEW YORK,

N. Y.

THE SCOT IN AMERICA.

BY PETER ROSS, LL. D.,

AUTHOR OF

"*Scotland and the Scots;*" "*Life of Saint Andrew;*" "*The Book of Scotia Lodge;*" "*Life and Works of Sir William Alexander, Earl of Stirling,*" *etc.*

In one volume, Crown 8vo. 460 pages, neatly bound in cloth. Price, $2.00.

THE RIGHT HON. W. E. GLADSTONE.

After reading "The Scot in America," the Right Hon. W. E. Gladstone, wrote to the author, Dr. Ross, as follows :
"The power which Scotland has exhibited beyond her own borders of contributing by her spare energies to enchance the social forces in other countries is a very noteworthy feature in the history of OUR race.

"PROGRESS," ST. JOHN, N. B.

"A mine of information to the public lecturer and after-dinner speaker who would exploit the Caledonian. From the preface to the closing chapter these 441 pages are packed with instances."

THE NEW YORK COMMERCIAL ADVERTISER.

"Dr. Ross is well known as an erudite and entertaining writer. His present work, 'The Scot in America,' is the result of many years' study and research. For the present it may rank as authoritative, nor is it at all likely to be superseded. The mass of material which he has sifted is immense. He is to be congratulated not only upon his talent as a historian, but as well upon his industry, a quality far rarer in these days of indifferent study."

WESTERN BRITISH-AMERICAN.

" 'The Scot in America,' is a new and interesting work from the pen of Peter Ross, LL. D., the well known authority on matters Scotch in the United States and Canada. Like all of Dr. Ross' previous literary efforts, 'The Scot in America' has an intrinsic merit and charm of diction that will be sure to win it a wide circulation among the patriotic and cultured Scots of America. * * * A wonderfully instructive and entertaining volume, well worthy the perusal of all Scottish Americans and should find a place in the library or parlor of every home."

THE POEMS OF GEORGE WILLIAMSON,

OF DETROIT, MICH.

ONE LARGE HANDSOME VOLUME.

Price $1.00.

SCOTTISH POETS IN AMERICA.

BY JOHN D. ROSS.

WITH BIOGRAPHICAL AND CRITICAL NOTICES.

One volume, 8vo., cloth, 225, pages, $1.50.

Contains sketches with poems of :

Thomas C. Latto, Duncan MacGregor Crerar, Prof. James C. Moffat, Hew Ainslie, Hon. William Cant Sturoc, William Lyle, James Kennedy, William Wilson, Andrew McLean, D. M. Henderson, Dr. John M. Harper, Robert Whittit, William McDonald Wood, Andrew Wanless, Alexander Wingfield, Malcolm Taylor, Jr., Evan McColl, William Murray, Alexander M'Lachlan, Gen. D. C. McCallum, John Patterson, William Telford, James D. Crichton, Donald Ramsay and John Massie, M. D.

A CLUSTER OF POETS.

SCOTTISH AND AMERICAN.

BY JOHN D. ROSS, LL. D.

Cloth. Illustrated. Nearly 400 pp. $1.50.

Contains sketches and poems of :

Rev. Duncan Anderson, M. A., William Anderson, Hon. Wallace Bruce, Hon. Chas. H. Collins, John Imrie, William T. James, James D. Law, Benjamin F. Leggett, Ph. D., Rev. Arthur John Lockhart, Rev. Burton W. Lockhart, D. D., Hunter MacCulloch, John Macfarlane, Hector Macpherson, Patrick Macpherson, George Martin, Charles Reekie, Robert Reid, Rev. Archibald Ross, Peter Ross, LL. D., Ralph H. Shaw, Rev. William Wye Smith, Albert E. S. Smythe and George Williamson.

CELEBRATED SONGS OF SCOTLAND.

EDITED BY JOHN D. ROSS.

From King James V. to Henry Scott Riddell. With Memoirs and Notes. One vol., 8vo, 400 pages, cloth, gilt top, $2.00.

☞This book is a great bargain. Order at once, as the few copies on hand will soon be bought up. Professor JOHN STUART BLACKIE once wrote to the Editor of it: "Your book or Scottish Song is a standard work of reference with me." This should be sufficient to convince Scotsmen that the book is A No. 1 in all respects.

ALL ABOUT BURNS.

COMPILED BY JOHN D. ROSS. LL. D.

Nearly 300 pages. Illustrations. Cloth, 75 cts., Paper 50 cts.

RANDOM SKETCHES ON SCOTTISH SUBJECTS.

BY JOHN D. ROSS.

Contains: Lady Nairne and her Songs, The Poet Fergusson, The Mother of Robert Burns, The Water Mill, etc. etc.

Cloth $1.00.

POMPEII—THE CITY OF DOOM.

BY BENJAMIN F. LEGGETT, PH. D.

Paper cover, 25 cents.

A SHEAF OF SONG.

BY BENJAMIN F. LEGGETT, PH. D.

12 mo., 154 pages, cloth, 50 Cents.

SAINT ANDREW.

THE DISCIPLE; THE MISSIONARY; THE PATRON SAINT.

BY PETER ROSS, Author of "Scotland and the Scots," etc.
Cloth, price $1.00.

THE LAST SCOTS PARLIAMENT.
A SKETCH OF THE PAST.

By A. MELVILLE. 66 pages, paper covers, 25 cents.

THE BURNS SCRAP BOOK.
COMPILED BY JOHN D. ROSS.

Full of choice Reading, Information, Anecdotes, Poems, etc.,
about ROBERT BURNS, his home, friends, country
and works. One volume, 256 pages,
Cloth, $1.00.

HOW I MADE MONEY AT HOME.

With the Incubator, Bees, Silkworms, Canaries, Chickens and
One Cow.

BY JOHN'S WIFE.

82 pp., illustrated. Price, 18 cents.

FROM DAWN TO DUSK.
By HUNTER MacCULLOCH.

16 mo., cloth, 134 pp. with Portrait. Contents: From dawn
to Dusk; Soliliquies; To My Wife; Miscellaneous;
Epigrams; Songs; Idyls of the Queen. 75 cts.

BESIDE THE NARRAGUAGUS AND OTHER POEMS.
By THE REV. ARTHUR JOHN LOCKHART,

112 pp., cloth, $1.00.

SCOTLAND AND THE SCOTS.
By PETER ROSS.

Author of "A Life of Saint Andrew," etc., etc.
Cloth, 245 pp. Price, $1.00.

THE BOOK OF SCOTIA LODGE.

By PETER ROSS.

Being the History of Scotia Lodge, No. 634, F. & A. M., New
York. Just published. Cloth, price, $1.50. Only
a few copies left.

THE NEW YEAR COMES, MY LADY, WITH OTHER POEMS.

By CHAS. H. COLLINS. 114 pp. Cloth, $1.00.

AN IDYLL OF LAKE GEORGE, AND OTHER POEMS.

By BENJAMIN F. LEGGETT, Ph. D.

Author of "A Tramp Through Switzerland," " A Sheaf of
Song," "The City of Doom," etc.

One volume, 12mo., Cloth, Price 75 cents.

ROBERT BURNS.

AN ODE ON THE CENTENARY OF HIS DEATH. 1796–1896.

By HUNTER MacCULLOCH.

32 pp. Illustrated. 8vo., Flexible cloth. Price 20 cents.

"Of the poems which the occasion has already produced,
none can well be more enthusiastic or elaborate than this ode."
—*London Spectator.*

"His flight is steady and sustained, never decending in
commonplace and frequently soaring to the serene heights
where the skylark sings."—*Brooklyn Times.*

BURNS' CLARINDA,

A COLLECTION OF ARTICLES CONCERNING BURNS' EDINBURGH HEROINE.

COMPILED BY JOHN D. ROSS, LL. D.

Cloth, $1.50.

www.ingramcontent.com/pod-product-compliance
Lightning Source LLC
Chambersburg PA
CBHW020614030726
47497CB00007B/2231